Welcome to Suite 4B!

Gone to the stables

Jina

Shh!! Studying—
please do not disturb!

Mary Beth

<u>GO AWAY!!!</u>

Andie

Hey, guys!
Meet me downstairs in the
common room. Bring popcorn!

Lauren

Join Andie, Jina, Mary Beth, and Lauren
for more fun at the Riding Academy!

And coming soon:

"You can't be serious!" Jina cried.

Jumping up from the sofa, Lauren hurried around the coffee table to stand by Mary Beth.

"Yes, she is serious," Lauren said. "And I am, too. Someone needs to stand up for the rights of all those poor, hunted foxes."

Andie shot Jina a horrified look. "I don't believe this!" She flopped back against the sofa cushions. "You two have really lost it. Jina, tell them they're nuts. Throw cold water on them. Lock them up in the barn. Do *something*."

Jina dropped her head in her hands. She had a hunch that tomorrow was going to be one big fat nightmare.

Foxhunt!

by Alison Hart

BULLSEYE BOOKS

Random House ⌂ New York

Special thanks
to the Gettys and
the Middlebrook Hounds

J
HAR

A BULLSEYE BOOK PUBLISHED BY RANDOM HOUSE, INC.

Copyright © 1995 by Random House, Inc., and Alice Leonhardt.
Cover design by Fabia Wargin Design and Creative Media Applica-
tions, Inc. Cover art copyright © 1995 by Dan Burr. All rights
reserved under International and Pan-American Copyright Conven-
tions. Published in the United States by Random House, Inc., New
York, and simultaneously in Canada by Random House of Canada
Limited, Toronto.

Library of Congress Catalog Card Number: 95-70810

ISBN: 0-679-87143-8

RL: 4.5

Manufactured in the United States of America

10 9 8 7 6 5 4 3 2 1

RIDING ACADEMY is a trademark of Random House, Inc.

"Okay, I have chips, sodas, hamburgers," Jina Williams checked aloud as she surveyed the kitchen counter, "rolls, pizzas, brownies, salad, popcorn…" Her voice trailed off.

Had she forgotten anything? She bit her lip. Her roommates would be here at her house any minute. It was the Friday after Thanksgiving, and Jina hadn't seen them in a week.

Butterflies fluttered in her stomach. Mary Beth, Lauren, and Andie were more than just her roommates, Jina had decided. They were the first good friends she had ever had, and she wanted tonight's sleep over to be perfect.

Maybe they'd rather have ice cream for dessert, she thought, rushing over to the freezer. She pulled open the door and surveyed the contents: one half gallon of chocolate marshmallow and a quart of strawberry. Would that be enough?

The ringing of the front doorbell made Jina jump. Slamming shut the freezer, she raced into the foyer of the condominium. Grandma Williams was already there, walking slowly toward the door. Her bent, arthritic fingers reached for the doorknob.

"I'll get it!" Jina hollered. She skidded on the marble tile in her stockinged feet, nearly knocking the elderly woman over.

"Jinaki Williams!" her grandmother scolded in her soft drawl. "You be more careful, child."

Jina grabbed the doorknob. "Sorry. I will." She gave her grandmother a big smile, hoping she would take the hint and disappear. Her roommates didn't need to know that until her mother came home, they were all going to be baby-sat by an eighty-two-year-old grandmother. But Grandma Williams placed her gnarled fingers on Jina's arm. "I can't wait to meet your new little friends. It seems like only yesterday I was pushing you through the park in your stroller." A tear formed in the corner of her eye.

Please don't cry, Jina pleaded silently.

The bell rang again. Jina whipped open the door.

"Jina!" Lauren Remick squealed. Dropping her overnight bag, the petite blonde leaped forward and gave Jina a huge bear hug. Mary Beth Finney, along with her nine-year-old brother, Benji, and Mr. Finney, stood stiffly in the outside hall, their arms filled with suitcases and sleeping bags.

"Boy, did I miss you!" Lauren gave Jina another squeeze.

Jina blushed. Even after living with Lauren at Foxhall Academy for three months, she still hadn't gotten used to her friend's affectionate enthusiasm. But she sure enjoyed it.

Jina opened the door wider so Mary Beth, her dad, and Benji could step into the foyer. Mary Beth grinned a happy hello. Jina grinned right back.

"Hello, Jina," Mr. Finney boomed. "It's nice to see you again."

"Hi, Mr. Finney." She shut the door. Benji and his dad looked just like Mary Beth—tall, red-haired, and freckled.

Turning, Jina introduced her grandmother.

"My, my, just look at you three girls. So grown-up." Mrs. Williams smiled wistfully.

"Why, I can remember when Jina here was in diapers. She used to—"

"Hey, Lauren!" Jina cut in, reaching for the boot bag slung over her roommate's shoulder. "Let me help you with your things."

Benji peered curiously down the long hall. "So this is where the famous Myra Golden lives," he said. "I've seen her on TV a couple of times. I really liked the show about the lady who said she served tea to Martians."

Jina nodded and took Mary Beth's riding helmet from Mr. Finney. She was so used to people wanting to know about her mother, a national talk show host, that weird comments didn't bother her anymore—much.

"Martians?" Grandma Williams frowned. "I don't believe I've seen any here in Baltimore."

"Your house is so beautiful," Lauren said. Hands clasped, she gazed at the fresh flowers on the antique table, the Oriental rugs on the dark wood floor, and the sparkling chandelier overhead.

"Uh, it's just a condo," Jina said quickly, picking up Lauren's overnight bag from the floor.

Benji snorted. "It's not *just* a condo. The button on the elevator said *penthouse suite.*"

"Sweets?" Grandma Williams took Lauren's hand and steered her down the hall toward Jina's bedroom. "Jina and I made brownies this afternoon. Oh, she's been so excited."

Mary Beth turned to her father. Standing on tiptoes, she gave him a peck on the cheek. "'Bye, Dad."

He gave her a hug, then handed her a small suitcase. "'Bye, sweetie. Call us when you know what time you need to be picked up."

Arms laden with stuff, Jina awkwardly shifted from foot to foot. Usually it didn't bother her when she watched other girls with their dads. But whenever holidays rolled around, she was all too aware that it was just her, her mom, and her grandmother.

"Give me a hug, too," Mary Beth said to Benji, her voice teasing as she reached for him.

"No way!" Benji made a disgusted face and pushed his older sister away.

When the Finneys left, Jina led Mary Beth down the hall to her room. A nervous lump rose in her throat. It had been a long time since she'd had friends over. What would they think of her room?

Jina stepped aside and Mary Beth walked in. There were two white canopy beds covered with flower-splashed spreads. Matching floor-length curtains framed the sliding glass doors that led to a balcony. On one side of the room was a shelf full of antique dolls. On the opposite side, next to an old-fashioned vanity, stood a two-story dollhouse complete with miniature furniture. Would her roommate think that was babyish?

"Cool room," Mary Beth declared instantly.

Jina let out her breath in relief.

Lauren was already standing on the balcony, hanging over the wrought-iron railing. "Hey, guys, come here and look at this!"

She waved excitedly for Jina and Mary Beth to join her. "You can see boat lights on the inner harbor and the masts of the *Constellation* and...how far up are we anyway?"

"Pretty high." Jina dumped the armful of things on one of the beds, then joined her friends on the balcony. "It's twelve stories."

Craning her neck, Mary Beth peered cautiously over the railing. "I can't believe your bedroom has its own balcony."

"The room was supposed to be a library," Jina explained, "but I asked my mom if I could have it instead."

"Smart move," Lauren said. She leaned

even farther over the rail, the wind whipping her blond hair around her cheeks. "You can see forever."

Mary Beth took a nervous step backward. "The only thing I see when I look out my window is the gray siding on the Pattersons' house next door."

Jina pointed to the left. "That's the National Aquarium and over on the right is Harborplace. It has lots of places to shop and eat."

"Wow." Lauren let out a low whistle. "We need to come back and sightsee someday."

"Maybe this summer you—" Jina began, but she was interrupted by the doorbell. "That must be Andie!"

Jina ran down the hall as the bell continued to ring. Someone was pressing way too hard.

Jina threw open the door. Andie Perez stared back at her, one hand on her hip. Her long curly dark hair was swirled around her shoulders like a storm cloud. "About time," Andie grumbled, pushing past Jina. Silently, she glanced around the foyer. "Are Mary Beth and Lauren here?" she asked, hardly looking at Jina.

"Yeah. They're in my room." Jina gestured down the hall.

But Andie was already heading for the bedroom. She wore a denim jacket over a heavy sweater and jeans with torn knees. A backpack was slung over one shoulder, and she carried a riding coat on a hanger.

Grandma Williams came up behind Jina and patted Jina's arm. "That's all right, dear. I'm sure she's just feeling shy."

"Did your dad come with you?" Jina asked when she caught up with Andie.

Andie nodded. "Yeah. But his new girl-friend was with him, so he rushed off," she added with a snort.

Stopping dead in the bedroom doorway, she surveyed the room. "Gee, Williams, aren't you a little old for dolls?"

Jina's heart sank.

"Andie, come here and check out the view," Lauren called from the balcony.

Andie dumped her things on the nearest bed and went out. Reluctantly, Jina trailed after her, a knot growing in her stomach.

I never should have invited her, she decided. She had almost forgotten how moody and sarcastic Andie could be. She'd probably find a zillion ways to ruin the sleep over.

"And over there is Harborplace and—"

Lauren was chattering on and on as if Andie cared.

Looking bored, Andie stood in the middle of the balcony, her hands jammed in her jeans pockets. "So how high up are we?"

Mary Beth grimaced. "Too high." She was huddled in front of the glass doors, her arms hugging her chest.

"I wonder if anyone ever tried to dive into the harbor from here," Andie said.

Lauren giggled nervously. "Don't joke about stuff like that."

Jina took a deep breath. Something was definitely bugging Andie.

"So your Thanksgiving didn't go too well, huh, Andie?" she said quietly.

Andie shrugged. "Not so great." Ducking her head, she stared down at her sneakers. "My dad worked most of the time and my old friends…" She shrugged again. "Well, you know, hanging around with them was really weird. I actually kind of missed you guys."

Jina bit back a smile. She couldn't believe Andie was admitting that. She glanced hesitantly at the others. "Me too. I missed all of you like crazy."

"Ditto," Mary Beth said. "I mean, I loved

9

seeing my family and all, but my brothers and sister were driving me crazy."

"Group hug! Group hug!" Lauren cried. She wrapped her arms around Jina and Mary Beth and herded them toward Andie. Mary Beth started giggling. "Quit tickling me, Remick!"

"Tickle? You want a tickle?" Andie joined in. Someone's fingers caught Jina in the ribs. She squirmed away, bumping into Mary Beth, who immediately lost her balance.

Laughing like hyenas, the four girls fell through the open doorway onto Jina's rug. Andie pulled a pillow off the bed and whacked Mary Beth.

Jina couldn't stop laughing.

Finally she began to relax. Tickling, pillow fights, hysterical giggling—her sleep over was going to be great!

2

"You know what I *really* miss?" Lauren said a few minutes later. The girls were sprawled on the rug, trying to catch their breaths.

"Let me guess—*Todd*," Mary Beth teased. She was lying perpendicular to Jina's feet.

"No, dummy." A pillow sailed through the air and landed on Mary Beth's stomach. "I miss Whisper."

"I know how you feel," Jina said. "I miss Superstar tons."

"Not as much as I miss Magic!" Andie said. "At least you get to foxhunt Whisper tomorrow, Lauren."

Lauren sighed. "I can't wait."

Andie propped herself up on one elbow. "You'd better be excited, because when we get back to Foxhall you won't be riding Whisper

11

anymore, remember? Mrs. Caufield assigned you that new horse, Fawn."

Jina grimaced. *Thanks for bringing that up, Andie.* She knew how upset Lauren was about having to switch school horses.

Abruptly, Jina sat up. "Is anyone hungry? We've got *tons* of food."

As if on cue, Grandma Williams poked her head into the room. Her short gray hair looked like a woolly ski cap. "Pizza's in the oven," she announced.

Mary Beth jumped to her feet. "Pizza! Yum. My favorite."

"So what's the gig for tonight, Williams?" Andie asked as she followed Jina down the hall. "Any of your mom's famous friends coming over?"

"Oooo!" Mary Beth gushed. She and Lauren were right behind them. "I'd love to meet Lance Leone, that soap opera guy who was on your mom's show Wednesday. Do you think he'll come over?"

"Sorry, guys." Jina glanced at Lauren and Mary Beth, hoping they weren't too disappointed.

"Oh," Mary Beth said. She definitely sounded disappointed.

12

"Besides, we should go to bed early," Jina continued. "We have to get up at six to get ready for the foxhunt."

"Go to bed early?" Lauren made a face. "No way."

Mary Beth punched Jina lightly on the arm. "Come on, Jina. No one ever goes to bed early at a sleep over."

"Hey, look at this." Andie had stopped in the arched doorway which opened into the living room.

She stepped into the room and waved her arm grandly. "And here we have the posh living room of famous TV star Myra Golden," she announced in a heavy British accent. "Where Ms. Golden and her lovely daughter, Jinaki, can spy on their neighbors"—she pointed to the picture window—"or watch themselves on TV." Turning, she gracefully flipped her hand toward the big-screen TV and entertainment center.

Lauren and Mary Beth burst out laughing. Even Jina had to grin. She had to admit, Andie *was* pretty funny.

"And when the effort of being famous wears out the darling duo, they can each relax on their own private sofa"—she gestured to the three white sofas grouped around an Oriental rug—"and gaze at their magnificent collection of African art arranged stunningly on the lighted shelves."

Andie struck a dramatic pose. Still laughing, the others applauded.

Mary Beth pointed to the huge TV. "Does your mom have private screenings—or whatever they're called—in here?"

"It's usually real late when my mom gets home," Jina explained. "The last thing she wants to do is watch TV. I got a video for us to watch later, though. *Black Beauty.*"

Andie started to gag. Before vacation, the girls had performed their original play, *Black Beauty's Hints,* in English class. They'd barely gotten a B.

Jina ignored Andie and beckoned for the girls to follow her. "Now you can see Myra Golden's famous kitchen. My grandmother's probably laid out a feast."

An hour later, they'd finished pigging out on pizza and hamburgers and french fries. Now they were scattered on the sofas in the living room, munching on popcorn and fudgy chocolate brownies.

"I'm stuffed." Andie let out a huge burp.

Mary Beth held up a brownie. "Deze aw dewicious," she mumbled, her mouth totally full.

"Before we start the video, I want to hear about everyone's vacation!" Lauren said eagerly. She had settled cross-legged on the sofa. "So, Mary Beth, did you see Brad?"

"Bwad?" Mary Beth started choking. Her face turned bright red and flecks of chocolate sprayed in the air.

"Gross, Finney." Andie moved out of the way.

Lauren ran over and pounded Mary Beth on the back. "Are you all right?"

"Here." Jina reached across the glass-topped coffee table and handed her a napkin.

Grabbing the napkin, Mary Beth nodded as she wiped her mouth. "I'm all right. I think."

"So what's the answer to the question?" Andie demanded. "Or are you too embarrassed to tell us?"

"No, no. I'll tell you." Mary Beth rubbed at the brownie crumbs on her jeans, her face still red. Finally, she took a deep breath and blurted, "Brad's going steady with Emily Zentz now, so I didn't even see him."

Andie snickered. "No big loss. He was a nerd."

"He was not!" Mary Beth flared.

"But you had a good time with your family," Lauren said hopefully. "Right?"

"Yeah." Mary Beth tossed the dirty napkin on the coffee table. "All my relatives came for Thanksgiving."

Lauren turned to Jina. "How about you, Jina? I bet you did something cool."

Jina stopped in mid-chew. Her roommates thought she led this glamorous life. How could she explain how boring the last week had been?

"Uh." She racked her mind for anything that might sound interesting. "Well, Kasey Jackson ate with us on Thanksgiving Day."

Mary Beth's jaw dropped. "The singer?"

"You know Kasey Jackson?" Even Andie seemed impressed.

Jina nodded.

"Did she sing for you?" Lauren asked.

"Or bring one of her totally gorgeous boyfriends with her?" Mary Beth added.

Jina shook her head. "Nope. She just spent the day with us."

"That's it?" the three chorused.

Disappointed, Lauren flopped back against the cushions, and Andie shoved more popcorn in her mouth. Jina glanced anxiously at her roommates. They were all starting to look bored.

Jumping up, she grabbed the video. "Boy, I can't wait for tomorrow," she said with exaggerated enthusiasm. "Foxhunting is so much fun. I hope everybody remembered their earmuffs and gloves."

"Tomorrow *is* going to be fun," Lauren agreed, "even though I'll only be hill-topping."

Mary Beth had a puzzled look on her face. "I'm hill-topping, too, right? Not that I know exactly what that is."

Andie chuckled. "It means you and Lauren will be with the little kids and old ladies, while Jina and I gallop through the fields leaping logs and coops."

"Whew." Mary Beth heaved a sigh. "I *hoped* that's what it meant. Dangerous Dan and I aren't ready for leaping any logs."

"Hill-topping is just as much fun," Lauren assured her. "The last time I went, the fox ran right in front of us. Then he disappeared into a barn." She giggled. "Of course, the

17

hounds totally lost the scent."

"I remember once when the fox zigzagged back and forth between the horses' legs," Andie said. "The hounds were so confused, they quit singing."

"What were they singing?" Mary Beth joked. "'Old MacDonald Had a Farm'?"

"Finney!" Looking disgusted, Andie threw a pillow at her. "That was so lame."

Jina put the video into the VCR, then stepped back to wait until the movie credits came on. Behind her, she could hear Lauren, Mary Beth, and Andie laughing together.

Okay, so the sleep over wasn't a major hit, Jina decided, but it wasn't a flop, either. And tomorrow she could quit worrying about being the perfect hostess. The foxhunt at Middlefield Stables would be super-fun for everybody.

When the movie started, Jina sat down next to Mary Beth.

"Well, I'm glad the fox outsmarts the hounds and gets away," Mary Beth was saying. She had the bowl of popcorn in her lap and was munching noisily.

"He's not always so smart," Andie said.

Mary Beth's hand froze halfway to her mouth. "What do you mean?"

Andie leaned forward, grinning an evil grin. Jina inhaled so fast she squeaked. She'd seen that expression before. It always meant trouble.

"I mean that sometimes the hounds catch the fox," Andie said in a low voice. "And when they do, you'd better cover your eyes, Finney. It's really gross."

Mary Beth gasped, popcorn slipping from her fingers. "You mean—the hounds *kill* the fox?"

Andie nodded. "Yep."

"Then forget the foxhunt tomorrow," Mary Beth exclaimed. She jumped up, and the bowl of popcorn spilled onto the floor. "I'm not going!"

"What do you mean you're not going on the hunt?" Jina repeated in disbelief. "You have to. I've arranged everything. Mrs. Caufield's bringing Dan for you to ride. I paid your capper's fee. And—and—" *And you'll ruin everything!*

Mary Beth stood on the other side of the coffee table, hands on her hips. "I can't go. Not if the fox gets killed."

Lauren threw a disgusted glance at Andie. "Andie was just trying to freak you out, Mary Beth. The hounds hardly ever catch the fox."

"But what if they do this time?" Mary Beth whirled to face her. "What if they catch him right in front of me? I'd throw up."

Jina groaned. She couldn't believe this was happening.

Andie rolled her eyes. "Come on, Finney. Foxes aren't so sweet and innocent. They kill cute little bunnies."

"For *food*!" Mary Beth declared hotly. "Not for sport. That's a big difference."

Just then the theme music from the video blasted on, and a giant-sized Black Beauty galloped across the screen. For the moment, everybody's attention switched to the movie.

Jina sat rigidly on the edge of the sofa, her brain whirling. What could she say to make Mary Beth change her mind? The hunt was supposed to be the highlight of the weekend. If Mary Beth didn't go, everything would be ruined.

She took a deep breath. "Mary Beth, Lauren's right. I've gone foxhunting about five times, and the hounds never caught a fox."

"Besides, what's the big deal if they do kill it?" Andie scoffed. "You eat meat, right? That hamburger we had tonight used to be some poor cow. And think of all those chickens that get chopped up to make chicken nuggets."

"That's disgusting!" Lauren sputtered.

Mary Beth crossed her arms in front of her chest. "I'm not going," she stated firmly. "I did a report on foxes in fourth grade. The father helps take care of the cubs. They live in families that love each other."

"Families?" Lauren squeaked, her blue eyes widening. "You mean the hounds might kill some poor cub's mommy or daddy?"

Andie threw up her hands in frustration. "No, goofball. By now, the babies are all grown-up."

"Still..." Lauren bit her lower lip. In the background, the music faded to a sad melody.

Great. Jina twisted her paper napkin between her fingers. Now Mary Beth had Lauren on her side. She had to do something.

"Okay, Mary Beth. We understand why you don't want to go." Jina tried again. "But you have to go. It's all arranged. You're my guest at Middlefield. Mrs. Caufield's vanning Dan to the stable for you. Besides, if you go, you'll see for yourself that we don't catch the fox."

"That's true." Staring into space, Mary Beth tapped her cheek as if deep in thought.

Does that mean I've convinced her? Jina wondered.

"You're right. I will go," Mary Beth announced.

Jina sighed in relief. *Thank goodness.*

"To protest the hunt!" Mary Beth jabbed

one finger in the air as the music from the video rose to a dramatic crescendo.

"What!" Andie bolted upright.

"That's right." Mary Beth grinned excitedly. "I'll make posters that say SAVE THE FOX and FOXES HAVE FAMILIES, TOO!"

"Y-you can't be serious!" Jina stammered.

Jumping up from the sofa, Lauren hurried around the coffee table to stand by Mary Beth. "Yes, she is serious," Lauren said, crossing her own arms in front of her chest. "And I am, too. Someone needs to stand up for the rights of foxes."

Andie shot Jina a horrified look. "I don't believe this!" She flopped back against the sofa cushions. "You two have really lost it. Jina, tell them they've lost it. Throw cold water on them. Have them locked up. Do *something*."

Jina opened and closed her mouth like a fish gasping. "I—I—I don't know what to do." On the screen, Black Beauty raced through the pouring rain to get help for his sick mistress.

"Do you have any posterboard and markers?" Mary Beth demanded. "Lauren and I need to get right to work."

Andie bounded off the sofa. "That does it.

I'm getting out of here. Jina, where's your bathroom?"

Numbly, Jina pointed toward the hall, and Andie stormed from the room.

"How about making a poster that says TAKE THE FOX OUT OF FOXHUNTING?" Lauren was suggesting to Mary Beth.

Jina dropped her head in her hands. *Why me?* she thought miserably.

"Hello, girls," a voice said.

Jina snapped her chin up. Her mother was standing in the doorway, the hall light illuminating her as if she were onstage. Myra's skin glowed golden brown, and her silver earrings glittered above the collar of her full-length fur coat.

"Having fun?" Jina's mother swept into the room, the coat flying behind her like Superwoman's cape.

Lauren opened her mouth, but nothing came out, and Mary Beth nodded as if she were in a daze. As usual, the glamorous Myra Golden had left Jina's friends speechless.

Hopping up from the sofa, Jina ran over to kiss her mother's cheek. "Hi, Mom. We were just watching *Black Beauty*, and—uh—talking about the foxhunt."

"It's nice to see you again, Ms. Golden," Lauren finally spoke up.

"Myra, please," Jina's mother corrected. "Did you girls eat yet? I know Jina and her grandmother were planning quite a feast." Putting her arm around Jina's shoulder, she drew her daughter closer. The fur tickled Jina's nose and made her sneeze.

"Hi, Ms. Golden," Andie said as she came back into the room. "Nice fur." She reached out and stroked the coat sleeve. "I wonder how many animals it took to make it," she added, smirking at Mary Beth.

Andie! Jina wanted to hiss, but she sneezed again instead.

Myra laughed heartily. "Absolutely none, dear. It's a faux fur. And call me Myra, please."

"Hey, Jina, maybe we could hunt a 'faux' fox tomorrow," Andie joked. "Then our roomies here wouldn't have to go through with their stupid protest."

Myra raised her brows. "Protest? Did I miss something?"

"Boy, did you," Andie said.

"Mom," Jina began hesitantly, "Mary Beth and Lauren want to make posters and protest tomorrow's foxhunt. But you know how conservative the members of the hunt are. Mr. Brink might have a heart attack. They might even kick me out of the hunt."

"Hmmm. A protest." Instead of rushing to Jina's rescue, Myra looked intrigued. Slipping off the fur coat, she settled comfortably on the sofa. "Come and sit down, honey," she said, patting the seat next to her. "I want to hear all about this."

Before Jina could take one step toward the sofa, Lauren, Andie, and Mary Beth rushed to sit beside Myra. Crowding around her, they all started talking at the same time.

"Mary Beth has this crazy—"

"Foxes take care of—"

"We need to make posters that—"

On and on they chattered until finally Andie asked, "Now don't you think a protest is a dumb idea, Myra?"

Say yes, Jina pleaded silently.

Cocking her head, Myra thought for a moment. "Well, no. Actually, I think a protest is a wonderful idea."

What? Jina gasped so hard she almost fell off the sofa.

Myra gave Lauren and Mary Beth an encouraging smile. "I admire your strong feelings, Mary Beth. You and Lauren are welcome to use any materials you can find in my office down the hall."

"Thanks!" Mary Beth beamed.

"But, Mom!" Jina protested. "This is Middlefield's big Thanksgiving hunt. Everyone will be furious!"

Myra gave a throaty chuckle. "You're right, Jina. All those stuffy members of the hunt will be horrified at the nerve of two adorable kids protesting the sacred sport of foxhunting."

Turning, Myra faced Lauren and Mary Beth, a gleam in her eye. "This calls for drastic measures. Girls"—she took both of their hands—"I'm calling my friend at the local TV station to have him send a crew to Middlefield. Tomorrow your protest will be on the news!"

"You're going to call the *news*?" Jina croaked. Maybe she hadn't heard her mother right. Maybe this was all just a bad dream.

"We'll be on TV?" Lauren and Mary Beth repeated excitedly.

Myra nodded. "*If* you're really serious about this protest."

"We are!" Grabbing each other's arms, Mary Beth and Lauren bounced on the cushions, shrieking.

Andie plugged her ears. "Would you two stop? You sound like a couple of pigs." Looking disgusted, she got up from the sofa and went over to look out the picture window.

"Jina?" Myra turned to her daughter.

"What?" Jina said, trying not to sound too

angry. As usual, her mother had taken every-thing over. She should have known her mom would think Mary Beth's idea was wonderful. It was almost as crazy as some of the shows she did on *Myra Golden Live*.

Jina's mother smiled. "Sweetie, will you show the girls where my office is and help them find the supplies they need? I'm going to change my clothes before I call the station."

"What about *Black Beauty*?" Jina asked, but Mary Beth, Lauren, and her mother were chattering so loudly they didn't hear her.

No, this isn't a bad dream, Jina decided glumly as she switched off the video. It was real. And she had a hunch that tomorrow was going to be one big fat nightmare.

"I bet we'll be the only ones arriving at Middle-field in a limousine," Mary Beth said the next morning. She was fiddling with the automatic ice maker built into the back of the limo's front seat.

It was early. All four girls were dressed in black hunt coats and buff breeches. Since it was cold, they wore long underwear and sweaters under their riding clothes. Their boots, gloves, and earmuffs were packed in the trunk as well as extra clothes for the after-hunt buffet.

"Oh, there might be another limo or two," Andie replied. She sat across from Jina, their knees almost touching. "Rich snobs love to hunt. But you and Lauren will definitely be the only ones carrying posters that say SAVE THE FOXES."

"And we'll be the only ones filmed for the TV news!" Lauren added excitedly. "We're going to be famous."

Andie shook her head. "Famous dopes."

Jina sighed and shifted her riding helmet to her other knee. *That's for sure*, she thought. *And everybody at Middlefield will blame me for inviting them.*

Mary Beth's stupid idea had ruined her sleep over. Now it was going to ruin the whole hunt.

Andie tugged at her choker. "When are we going to get there? I feel like a stuffed turkey with all these clothes on."

"Soon," Jina replied, glancing out the tinted window. The rising sun was half hidden by gray clouds.

Snow? she wondered. Probably. The way

things looked, it was going to storm buckets.

Lauren tapped her on the shoulder. "Are you okay? You're kind of quiet this morning."

Turning, Jina tried to smile. It was nice *someone* had noticed. "Sure. I'm okay. I'm looking forward to the hunt, even if you guys aren't."

"Oh, we're looking forward to it," Mary Beth proclaimed. "Especially since Lauren and I decided the best way to help the fox is to hilltop ourselves. That way we can keep an eye on him and make sure he doesn't get caught."

Andie burst out laughing. "What are you going to do? Throw yourself in the middle of the hounds?"

Lauren pressed her lips together. "Laugh all you want, Andie. We don't care."

"Middlefield up ahead," Charles, the driver, announced over the intercom. All four girls craned their necks, trying to get a better view as the limo made a left turn.

Rolling pastures stretched on both sides of the curving driveway. Run-in sheds dotted the pastures, and a few blanketed horses grazed on the frost-covered grass.

At the top of the hill stood Middlefield's huge green-and-white barn and indoor arena.

A dozen horse trailers and vans were parked in front of the buildings.

"There's Foxhall's horse van," Lauren said eagerly. "That means Whisper is here already."

Lauren, Mary Beth, and Andie were riding Foxhall horses. Jina was borrowing a horse that belonged to another client of her trainer, Todd Jenkins.

"Hey!" Mary Beth said excitedly. "The camera crew's here, too."

Jina looked in the direction her roommate was pointing. A utility van with KLZ-TV written on the side was parked among the horse trailers. A woman in black pants and a tailored hound's-tooth jacket stood next to it, talking to a man wearing a formal scarlet hunt coat, top hat, and white breeches.

It was Mr. Brink, the master of foxhounds. Jina sunk lower in her seat, hoping he wouldn't see her.

"Ooo, I'm getting nervous, Mary Beth." Lauren clutched her stomach. "Maybe this protest wasn't such a good idea. I'd forgotten what a big deal a hunt is."

"We can't back out now," Mary Beth told her, but she didn't sound so sure of herself now, either.

Andie leaned closer to Lauren as if she were going to tell her a secret. "You should be worried," she said in a low voice. "The whippers-in don't like anyone interfering with their hounds. You know what I mean?" She snapped her hand as if cracking a whip.

Lauren's cheeks paled, and she gave Mary Beth a worried look.

"Whippers-in?" Mary Beth said nervously. "What are those?"

"Forget it," Jina said with a sigh. "You don't want to know."

Charles slowed the limo, then pulled in next to the Foxhall van. "We're here, ladies."

"There's Dorothy." Andie waved excitedly to an older woman currying a chestnut horse. Dorothy Germaine was Foxhall's barn manager and assistant instructor.

Lauren squealed. "That's Whisper she's brushing. Whisper! It's me!" Throwing open the door, she pushed past Jina's knees and jumped from the limo.

Cold air rushed in. Jina shivered as she climbed out after Andie. Charles had opened the door on the other side for Mary Beth. He stood at attention beside it, the silver buttons on his uniform gleaming in the early light.

"Thank you," Mary Beth said, looking at the driver in surprise.

"You're welcome." He bowed at the waist, then went around to open the trunk for Jina.

"Now you be careful, Miss Jina," he warned in his soft voice. "Galloping around those woods can be dangerous."

"I will." Jina smiled reassuringly at him. Charles was about as old as Grandma Williams. He had been the family chauffeur for as long as she could remember.

She gathered up her things. "Lauren, Andie, here are your boots!" she called. But Lauren was too busy cooing over Whisper to hear her, and Andie had disappeared inside the van.

"I'll take the posters," Mary Beth said, pulling them carefully out of the trunk.

"And I'll take care of everything else." Charles patted Jina's shoulder. "You go find your horse."

"Thanks." Jina turned, plowing right into Mary Beth's back. Her roommate was staring at a woman dressed in a shad-bellied hunt coat, canary breeches, and top hat. "Wow. Is that Mrs. Caufield?"

Jina nodded. Mrs. Caufield was the director

of Foxhall Academy's riding program. "Every year she dresses formally for the Thanksgiving hunt. Dorothy told me."

Mary Beth swallowed hard. "Oh, boy. She's not going to be too happy about our protest."

You've got that right, Jina wanted to say.

"But I'm going to do it anyway," Mary Beth said, clutching the posters to her chest. "Right. Well, see you later."

Jina hurried off to find Todd. Maybe if she stayed far enough away from Mary Beth and Lauren, no one would realize that they were her guests.

Middlefield's large barn was bustling with activity. Jina walked down the tanbark-covered aisle, ducking under crossties. Todd was tacking up a handsome bay gelding.

"Hey, Jina!" he greeted her. Jina's trainer was in his mid-twenties. His blond hair was hidden by his helmet, and he was already dressed in his hunt clothes. "Your mount's over there in stall twelve. His name's Geoffrey. I brushed him, but you'll have to tack him up."

"Thanks, Todd." Jina peered into the stall, and a chestnut with four white socks pressed his muzzle against the wire-mesh door. He had a Roman nose, and despite his attractive color, Jina thought he was kind of homely.

"He's a real sweetheart like Superstar," Todd added.

But not nearly as beautiful. Jina felt a pang of sadness. In September, her horse, Superstar, had bowed a tendon at a show. It had been over two months since she'd ridden him, and she really missed it.

"Jina! Jina! Jina!" a shrill voice rang out. A small whirlwind of a girl ran up and grabbed Jina around the waist, practically knocking her over.

Jina caught herself on the stall door. "Hi, Whitney. What are you doing here?"

Whitney beamed up at her, her black helmet hiding most of her face. "I'm foxhunting, you silly!" she exclaimed. "Me and Applejacks!"

"You are?"

Behind her, Todd stifled a laugh. They both knew what a pain Whitney could be sometimes.

"She's hill-topping," Todd corrected.

"Oh," Jina said relieved. "Mary Beth and Lauren are hill-topping, too."

Whitney's mouth rounded in an O. "They

are? Oh, goody! Where are they? I want to see them."

Jina pointed to the doors at the end of the barn. Whitney dashed down the aisle, dodging horses and tack boxes. "They're carrying a bunch of posters," Jina called after her.

Todd came up beside her. "Posters?"

Jina sighed. "Don't ask. So where's Geoffrey's bridle?"

Fifteen minutes later, Jina was mounted and riding down the aisle. Several kids she knew waved to her as Geoffrey strode from the barn.

As they approached the field—the group of mounted riders who were participating in the hunt—Jina's pulse quickened. The scarlet coats of the master, huntsman, and whippers-in stood out against the gray sky. Many of the members were wearing hunt colors, and some were dressed in formal shad-bellied coats and top hats. All of them were riding sleek horses that pranced and pawed with anticipation.

Then the yelping sound of excited hounds filled the air. The kennelman had opened the trailer door, and the hounds leaped to the ground in a stream of brown, black, and white.

Tooot. The huntsman gave one long blast on

his horn, and the hounds ran to him, milling around his horse's legs.

Geoffrey's ears pricked, and goose bumps raced up Jina's arms. She'd almost forgotten how much she loved to hunt.

Then she heard another noise over the hounds—three voices, shouting in unison. Jina spun in the saddle. Mary Beth, Lauren, and Whitney were marching around the corner of the barn, posters held high in the air.

"Save the foxes! Save the foxes!" they chanted. "Animals have rights too!"

5

Jina watched in dazed silence as Mary Beth, Lauren, and Whitney marched toward the field of riders, waving their posters like flags. Everyone stopped what they were doing to stare at them in surprise.

"Jina!" Andie called as she trotted up. Since Magic was still too green to hunt, she was riding a big-boned bay, Ranger. A wild strand of hair had escaped from Andie's helmet, and it flopped up and down as she posted. "Can you believe those dorks are going through with their stupid protest?"

Slowly, Jina shook her head.

"And what is Whitney doing with them?" Andie added, halting her horse beside Geoffrey.

"I don't know." Jina pressed her fingers

against her eyes, hoping the protesters would stop. But their shouts only grew louder.

"Foxhunting unfair to foxes!" she heard Mary Beth holler.

"Foxes have families!" Lauren chimed in.

"Foxes are cute!" Whitney flapped her poster and several horses bolted.

Andie groaned. "Great. Here comes your mom's cameraman. Doesn't he have anything more important to shoot—like a murder?"

Jina twisted in the saddle. The reporter in the hound's-tooth jacket was hurrying toward the protesters, a cameraman jogging behind her.

"Uh-oh," Andie said dramatically, her eyes widening. Jina whirled to see what she was talking about.

Mr. Brink, the master of foxhounds, was riding toward Mary Beth and Lauren from the other direction. As he trotted past on his horse, Jina caught a glimpse of his face. It was as scarlet as his hunt coat.

Andie grinned gleefully. "This protest stuff might be fun after all. Wanna ride over and catch the fireworks?"

"No way. And don't you mention my name,

either," Jina warned. "I don't want to have any part of this."

Andie shrugged and turned Ranger toward the gathering group. "Okay. But don't be jealous when we're on tonight's news and you aren't," she called over her shoulder.

The reporter was talking to Mary Beth and Lauren. Whitney was behind them, dancing around. Giggling, she shook her poster at several more horses. Jina heard Mr. Brink bellow as his horse slid to a stop, then wheeled with fright.

"Whitney!" Dorothy stormed across the drive and yanked the poster from Whitney's grasp. At the same time, Mrs. Caufield rode up on T.L., another Foxhall horse.

Jina gulped. Part of her felt sorry for Lauren and Mary Beth. From the look on the riding director's face, they were in big trouble.

But another part of her was still mad at them. No one had forced them to stage this stupid protest. No one had asked them to ruin the hunt.

"Let's get out of here," Jina whispered to Geoffrey. Gathering the reins, she guided him toward the hounds. They were bedded down beside the huntsman's horse, waiting patiently for the signal to move off.

"What's going on?" Todd called, riding up. Jina pulled her helmet lower on her forehead. She was too embarrassed to look at him.

"Um, Mary Beth and Lauren decided to protest killing the fox," she explained, keeping her voice low.

"Killing what fox? We've never killed a fox."

"Shhh." Jina glanced around, hoping no one had heard him. "I know that."

Todd halted his horse, Court Jester, who pawed the gravel as if to say let's go. Jina figured Jester was about twenty-five years old. Todd had shown him successfully for years, but ever since he'd retired him from the show ring, the old gray was addicted to foxhunting.

Last year, during a January hunt, Todd had left Jester behind because he'd seemed stiff in the hind legs. But Jester had had other ideas. Jumping over the pasture fence, he'd trotted spryly down the road to join the field as they'd headed down the drive.

"Well, it looks like their big protest just got canceled," Todd observed.

Jina turned to look. Dorothy was hustling Mary Beth and Lauren away from the field, her large hands firmly on their shoulders. The reporter was saying something to Mr. Brink, who angrily stabbed his finger in the direction of the girls. Then, the master abruptly spurred his horse and cantered toward the waiting field. When he passed by Jina, he glanced her way, his face still beet red.

Jina grimaced. *He must have found out that Mary Beth and Lauren were my guests.*

"Moving off!" the master yelled.

The huntsman picked up his horn, and the hounds immediately scrambled to their feet. *Da-dup, da-dup, da-dup*, he blew as he led them through a wide gate and into the back pasture. The two whippers-in, their whips hanging at the horses' sides, followed the pack.

"We're off!" Todd said. "Finally."

Jina took one last look behind her. Mary Beth and Lauren had disappeared around the corner of the barn. Since they were hill-topping—if they'd even be allowed now—they'd be going with a separate group.

Jina held Geoffrey back until the master and senior hunt members rode past. She'd be riding last with the other juniors.

"You missed it, Williams," Andie said as she steered Ranger beside Geoffrey. "The master chewed out our two idiot roommates." She snickered. "It'll make the news for sure."

"Let's hope not," Jina muttered, halting Geoffrey to let another rider through the gate. When she urged him forward, he strode calmly after the other horses.

Ranger, his neck already sweaty, danced sideways. Andie had to scoot her leg forward to keep from hitting the fence post.

"Who's the field master today?" Andie asked. Standing in her stirrups, she tried to see the front of the field. There were about thirty riders in all, strung in a line as they headed for the covert—the area that would be hunted.

"It's Mr. Brink, so don't do anything stupid," Jina warned. She was in enough trouble already.

"Me? Do something stupid?" Andie said innocently.

Fifteen minutes later, the field reached the edge of a partially wooded area that was thick with brambles and high grass. Mr. Brink raised his arm, signaling the riders to halt their horses.

Jina craned her neck, trying to see. The huntsman and whippers-in were working the hounds on the other side of a log jump that had been built into the pasture fence. Jina glimpsed flashes of brown and white as the hounds ran back and forth, hunting for the scent.

Suddenly, all the hounds opened up and, noses to the ground, raced from the thicket and up the hill. The huntsman and whippers-in charged after them. Jina figured they must have picked up a hot scent.

Leading the field, the master jumped his horse over the logs. The other members followed one by one.

Beside Jina and Geoffrey, Ranger crow-hopped in place until it was his turn, then he bounded toward the fence. Geoffrey flicked his ears and tossed his head. He was ready to go, too.

Jina guided Geoffrey toward the fence, the chilly wind slapping her cheeks. The stack of logs, solid and high, suddenly loomed in front of her.

Her heart flew into her throat. Geoffrey didn't hesitate a second, leaping over the logs as if they weren't even there. He landed easily in the mud on the other side, then galloped up the hill.

Tingles of excitement ran up Jina's arms. Leaning forward, she moved with her horse. His powerful hindquarters churned as they raced up the hill, the yelps of the hounds floating down to them like music.

Mary Beth and Lauren don't know what they're missing, Jina thought. *Foxhunting is the best!*

A light snow began to fall as Jina and Geoffrey skimmed across the rolling pasture. Flakes blew into Jina's face, melting instantly where they landed.

The wind rushed past, stinging her cheeks. Then she heard the sudden pounding of hooves. She peered sideways to see who was coming up beside her.

"Isn't this cool?" Andie shouted.

Jina flashed her a smile. "Definitely!" she hollered back, but Ranger, foam spraying from his mouth, had already pulled ahead.

The master slowed to a trot. Jina gripped the reins, wondering what was going on. Then she realized she couldn't hear the hounds any-more.

The field halted on the crest of the hill.

Below them, in the misty valley, the hounds worked the scent. Noses to the ground, they trotted back and forth, silently searching for the line.

About ten minutes later, one hound began to open up. The others froze, listened, then honored the first hound by running to where he was working the scent.

Immediately, they began to chorus. Tails wagging, they charged back up the hill.

Geoffrey pranced sideways. All around Jina, horses danced and threw their heads up. A few bucked in place or kicked out, furious at having to wait.

Jina circled Geoffrey toward a hedgerow, trying to settle him. A rustle of dry leaves, then a flash of red caught her eye. Stopping dead, Geoffrey stared suspiciously into the bushes.

Jina peered closer. Ten feet in front of her, the fox was weaving through the hedgerow, his bushy tail the only thing that gave him away. Slowly, Jina reached up to take off her helmet and point it at the tangle of brush, signaling that she had spotted the fox.

But her hand froze on the brim as Mary Beth's words rang through her head—*Foxes have families!*

Then the hounds bounded toward her, heading for the hedgerow. Geoffrey danced in place as they swarmed past his legs. Jina grabbed mane with one hand while holding tightly to the rein with the other.

The hounds crashed into the hedgerow, singing excitedly, the brambles ripping at their faces and ears. Then, just as quickly, they took off down the hill after the fleeing fox.

Jina exhaled with relief as the rest of the field followed. Andie cantered by, laughing, and Todd waved her on with an encouraging smile.

Jina trotted after them. Despite the cold, she was drenched with sweat.

At the bottom of the hill, horses and riders jumped a muddy stream lined with heavy brush and fallen trees. Upstream, thick cedars covered the hillside. Downstream, the hounds, at a loss, zigzagged in and out of the icy water, searching for the scent.

After ten minutes, the huntsman was about to blow his horn, signaling the hounds back to him, when a red streak burst from a hollow log. Tail straight out, the fox raced for the cedars. The hounds took off after him.

The master raised his arm, telling the riders

not to follow. The cedars were too thick.

The music from the hounds echoed through the trees. Waving his arm, the master directed the field to the right of the cedars. A woven-wire fence ran down the hillside. On the other side was a snow-dusted pasture. A coop had been built into the fence.

One after another, horses and riders flew over the coop, then tore up the hill. When Jina and Geoffrey reached the top, Jina was breathing hard and Geoffrey's neck was dark with sweat. The master pulled up his horse. The other riders stopped, too, and listened for the hounds.

They stood, waiting for what seemed like forever, trying to locate where the hounds had gone. Jina shivered as the cold crept under her sweater, chilling her damp skin.

Then the faint sound of hounds reached her ears. It was coming from the woods to their right.

Jina twisted in the saddle, half expecting to see the fox escaping again into the cedars. Instead, a group of riders trotted from the woods. It was the hill-toppers.

Jina waved to Mary Beth and Lauren. Mary Beth was riding Dan, the super-quiet horse she used for lessons at Foxhall. Lauren rode beside her on Whisper, a small chestnut mare. Behind them, Whitney was on Applejacks, her gray pony, and Dorothy rode on Windsor, another Foxhall lesson horse.

"Yoo-hoo!" Whitney called, until a sharp "hush!" from Dorothy shut her up.

Lauren and Mary Beth both waved. Jina hoped they were having fun.

The singing of the hounds grew closer. "This way!" the master called. He led the field across the pasture at a brisk canter, leaving the hill-toppers far behind.

As they approached another jump, every-one slowed to a trot. Horses and riders bunched before a stone wall built into a three-board fence.

Jina deepened her seat and took a firm hold on the reins. On the other side of the fence was a wooded area. She remembered from a past hunt that it was full of streams, rocks, and steep embankments. Geoffrey didn't need to go crashing over the wall and into trouble.

Ahead of her, Andie circled Ranger. Andie had tightened her hold, and Jina saw her reach down to pat Ranger's lathered neck. But the big horse was fighting the reins, eager to gallop off.

Jina guided Geoffrey next to Ranger. "Try staying behind me," she called to Andie. "Geoffrey's really laid back. Maybe he'll help calm Ranger."

Andie nodded once.

When all the other horses had jumped, Jina turned Geoffrey toward the stone wall. She held him to a trot until the horse and rider in front of her had disappeared into the woods. Behind her, she could hear Andie crooning, "Whoa, Ranger. Easy, buddy."

Squeezing her calves against Geoffrey's sides, Jina urged him into a canter. His ears flicked twice as he approached the wall, and his muscles tensed in anticipation.

Suddenly, Ranger burst past, cutting right in front of Geoffrey. Jina pulled hard on the left rein, trying to avoid running into the board fence that flanked the wall. Geoffrey swerved sharply, pitching Jina sideways. Her foot flew from the stirrup. At the last second, she caught his mane and pulled herself back into the saddle.

Looking back over her shoulder, she glimpsed Ranger barreling full speed toward the jump. Andie had given up trying to stop him. Grabbing mane, she held on as Ranger flew over the fence and into the woods.

Jina heard the sound of branches cracking and brush snapping. Her fingers tensed on the reins. *Was Andie all right?*

Jina found her stirrup, then circled and approached the wall again. Her heart was hammering in her chest. Geoffrey leaped over it, immediately slowing to a trot. "Andie!" Jina called urgently. Geoffrey jogged into the thick woods, carefully dodging trees and brambles. A branch slapped Jina's helmet.

Frantically, she hunted right, then left. There was no sign of Ranger or Andie.

That means she's okay, Jina reassured herself. *She got over the jump safely and caught up with the field.*

Her heart slowed as she steered Geoffrey to the muddy, trampled trail. She knew she wasn't far behind the field, but the swirling snow made it hard to see.

Suddenly, Geoffrey skidded to a halt. Throwing his head up, he peered wide-eyed into the woods.

"What is it?" Jina whispered. With a snort, the horse backed up a step. Pulling the reins from her hands, he ducked his head and blew noisily at a pile of fresh manure.

It was then that Jina saw the hoofprints veering off from the others. She followed them with her gaze. *Why had someone ridden into the woods?* she wondered. Then she noticed the trail of red drips, like paint splashed in the snow.

Andie!

An image of her friend, staggering into the woods, dazed and bleeding, filled Jina's mind. She clapped a hand over her mouth, suppressing a cry.

Wait, that's not right. She lowered her hand. *Hoof*prints were zigzagging into the woods, not *foot*prints. And from the depth of the print, Jina could tell the horse had been moving fast.

Too fast for the woods.

Jina inhaled sharply. Had her roommate smacked into a tree? Quickly, Jina gave herself a shake. Imagining horrible scenes wasn't going to help.

Cupping one hand to her mouth, she called again, "Andie!"

"Over here!" came the answering cry, and Jina was flooded with relief.

Raising his head, Geoffrey nickered. A horse nickered in reply. Jina steered Geoffrey into the woods, ducking and dodging branches as they followed the hoofprints.

Finally, she spotted Andie and Ranger walking toward them. Andie had dismounted and was leading her horse by the reins. When Ranger saw Geoffrey, he let out an earsplitting bellow. Jina was glad to see that Andie wasn't dazed and bleeding—just furious.

"What happened?"

Andie scowled over her shoulder at Ranger. "The big jerk went nuts. He charged into the woods like a runaway train. It's lucky I didn't get whacked in the head by a branch."

"Are you all right? I saw blood."

"I'm fine. But Ranger busted open that old wound on his hock. Remember when he cut it in the trailer at the horse show?"

Jina nodded. "Is he lame?"

"No. I think he just knocked off the scab. But he shouldn't be charging around anymore like a wild mustang. I'll have to take him back to Middlefield."

"Oh."

Jina must have looked disappointed because Andie said quickly, "You don't have to come with me. I can find my way back."

"No, I'll go with you," Jina said. She circled Geoffrey and followed Ranger back to the trampled path. "Wait here. I'll ride ahead and tell the master we're going back. Let's hope they didn't get too far."

Andie nodded. She was standing by Ranger's left flank, inspecting his hock. "Yeah. Looks like he knocked off the scab."

It took Jina about ten minutes of trotting to catch up with the field. They had stopped on the other side of the woods. Huddled in a group, they were listening for the hounds.

Jina spotted Mrs. Caufield. The top of the director's hat was sprinkled with snow, and the tip of her nose was red with cold.

Between breaths, Jina explained what had happened.

"I'll tell the master," the riding director said, keeping her voice low. "Do you know how to get back to Middlefield?"

Jina nodded. "I've been on trail rides out here before."

"Tell Andie she needs to hose Ranger's leg and then wash it gently with some sterile

57

gauze squares. They're in the medical kit in the front of the van."

Jina nodded again.

"Are you sure you'll be okay?" the director repeated, frowning worriedly.

"Positive. Besides, Dorothy and the hill-toppers were right behind us. If Ranger's not lame, maybe we'll join them for a while."

"That sounds like a good idea." Mrs. Caufield smiled, then glanced over her shoulder. The rest of the riders were moving off down the hill. "See you back at Middlefield," she said, touching the brim of her top hat as T.L. spun to join the others.

Geoffrey started after T.L., eager to get on with the chase.

"Whoa, buddy." Jina tugged gently on the reins. Tucking his chin, he halted, but the flick of his ears told her that he wanted to go with them.

"Me too." With a sigh, she patted his neck. "You're a good guy, Geoffrey. Any other horse would be trying to dump me so he could join his buddies. Maybe you aren't as gorgeous as Superstar, but Todd was right—you're just as sweet."

Jina turned her mount toward the woods.

In the distance, the blast of the huntsman's horn told her something exciting was happening. Confused, Geoffrey sidestepped away from the woods.

Jina pressed her calf against his right side, forcing him to move left, then forward. Geoffrey tossed his head once in protest, then strode into the woods. Jina was glad she didn't have to fight with him. It was bad enough having to quit in mid-hunt.

For a few minutes, they walked along in silence. The snow, damp and heavy now, coated twigs and branches like frosting.

A rabbit skittered from under a log and raced into the woods. A cardinal, vivid red against the white snow, fluttered out of a bush.

Jina grinned. She'd never been on a trail ride by herself before. It was pretty cool.

Pretty *cold*, she decided. Now that she and Geoffrey weren't galloping full tilt, her toes and fingers were growing numb.

She kicked her feet out of the stirrups. She rotated both her ankles, then wiggled her toes inside her boots. When a little warmth flowed back into her feet, she worked on her fingers, tucking one hand at a time inside her coat.

Beginning to feel better, Jina stuck her feet

back in her stirrups. Then she relaxed deep in the saddle and gazed around her.

With its cloak of white, the woods seemed magical. When she was foxhunting, Jina hadn't had time to enjoy the sights and sounds of the woods. Now she could hear the whisper of the falling snow, the twitter of birds, and the rap of a distant woodpecker.

"There you are!" Andie's booming voice cut into Jina's thoughts. She was leading Ranger toward them. When the bay saw Geoffrey, he whiffled excitedly.

"I thought maybe Ranger and I would have to rescue *you*," Andie said. The shoulders of her hunt coat were wet with snow, and Ranger's forelock was white. "What took you so long?"

"I was just looking around. I told Mrs. Caufield we were going back to the barn."

Andie jabbed her thumb in the direction of Ranger's hind leg. "He's not lame. In fact, he almost dragged me down the path trying to catch up with you. But I guess it only makes sense to go back." Her shoulders slumped, and she seemed as crestfallen as Jina.

"I told her we might join the hill-toppers too," Jina said, hoping to make her feel better.

"What? And rescue foxes?" Andie shook her head. "No way am I associating with those kooks."

"Dorothy's with them. You know she wouldn't let Mary Beth and Lauren do something stupid."

"That's true." Andie thought for a moment as she ran down her stirrup. "Okay. If we see them, we can hang out with them a little while. But they better not go diving down foxholes in some kind of commando mission."

Jina laughed, and Andie lowered her stirrup so she could mount the tall Ranger. But as soon as she stuck her toe in the iron, he lunged forward. She clung to the pommel, halfway on and halfway off.

"Whoa, Ranger!"

Striding toward Geoffrey, Ranger touched noses and squealed. Andie hung on to the pommel and cantle for a second, then pulled herself into the saddle.

"Whew," she puffed, her cheeks bright red. "Hunting this guy is work." Gathering the reins, she made him back up, then halt. "Now you *stand* here," she said gruffly.

"Didn't Mrs. Caufield hunt him last year?" Jina asked.

"Yeah. I guess he must have been fine then, or she wouldn't have let me ride him today," Andie said as she readjusted her stirrup.

When she had finished, she turned Ranger and led the way down the trail. Geoffrey ambled behind on a loose rein. Jina stuck out her tongue and caught a cluster of snowflakes. When they melted, she smiled to herself.

Okay, so she'd only gotten to hunt for a couple of hours. But just fooling around in the woods was fun, too.

For the last three years, she'd concentrated so hard on showing, she hadn't had time for many leisurely trail rides. She'd never realized what she'd been missing.

Andie turned in the saddle. "So are you still mad at Lauren and Mary Beth?"

Jina frowned. *Was she?* "Umm," she stalled, not sure about her answer.

"You were pretty bent out of shape last night. Not that I blame you. Mary Beth did ruin our slumber party. I mean, *I* would have *loved* to have finished watching *Black Beauty*."

Jina flushed. *So Andie had had a lousy time, too.*

"And your mom," Andie continued. "Whew. She was so excited by Mary Beth's protest, I thought she was going to invite her to come on one of her shows." She waved her arm in an arc. "I can see the title now, 'Dumb People Who Protest Dumb Things.'"

Only my mother didn't think it was so dumb, Jina wanted to say.

An unexpected rush of anger made her grasp the reins tightly. Then it dawned on her why she was so mad.

It wasn't just because of Mary Beth and Lauren. Sure, her roommates had ruined the sleep over and made fools of themselves—at the foxhunt. But that was nothing compared to the way her mother had fussed over her roommates—like they were the most important people in the world.

And she totally ignored me, Jina thought glumly. Her mother had gotten more excited over her friends' stupid protest than *anything* Jina had ever done.

A warm tear slid down Jina's cheek. Quickly, she wiped it away.

Quit feeling sorry for yourself, Williams, she scolded herself. She knew her mother loved her. She just wasn't sure *why.* She wasn't anything like charming, sweep-them-off-their-feet Myra Golden. And she definitely wasn't gutsy and outgoing like the great protesters, Lauren and Mary Beth. She was too serious and, well, *boring.*

Jina blew out her breath. Maybe she was more like her father. She'd probably never know. She'd never even met him.

"Are you all right?" Andie asked, staring at her curiously as they emerged from the woods. Andie halted Ranger in front of the stone wall.

Geoffrey stopped next to him. "Yeah." Jina

ducked her chin. There was no way she wanted to talk about parents with Andie, even though her roommate would probably understand better than anyone.

"Are you going to make Ranger jump the wall again?" Jina asked instead.

"Yup. Quietly, this time. And no racing off into the sunset, either."

"You won't have to worry about a sunset today. It's snowing too hard."

"That's for sure."

For a moment, the two of them gazed at the heavy dark clouds and swirling flakes. At least an inch of snow had covered the grass by now, and a cold wind was blowing across the pasture. Jina shivered. Her hunt coat and sweater didn't seem so warm anymore.

"Well, let's get over this wall and find the hill-toppers," Andie said, urging Ranger into a trot.

This time, Ranger sailed smoothly over the wall, coming to a dead stop as soon as Andie commanded, "Whoa."

Geoffrey flew over right after him, but Jina kept cantering. Grinning, she galloped along the crest of the hill feeling as free as the wind. With a whoop, Andie raced after her. When they reached the cedars, Jina finally pulled up.

"Whew! That was fun!" Andie puffed. She twisted to check Ranger's hock.

"It looks okay," Jina assured her.

Andie bit her lip. "Yeah. I still shouldn't have raced him like that," she admitted guiltily.

"Hallo-o-o!" A voice called.

"Hallo-o-o!" Several voices echoed right after it.

Jina spun in her saddle as seven snow-covered riders trotted out of the woods. Slowing, they filed through the gate built next to the stone wall.

"It's the hill-toppers!" Andie cupped her hands around her mouth. "Hallo-o-o!" she called back.

"Jina! Andie!" Whitney's enthusiastic cry shot across the valley. Bouncing as she posted, the little girl trotted briskly down the hill on her gray pony, Applejacks.

Jina had to laugh. She didn't know what was moving faster—Whitney's bottom or Apple's short legs.

"Jina! Andie!" Whitney cried again as she jounced toward them. "We saw the hounds. We saw a dead deer. We saw some cows!"

"That's great," Jina called. Behind Applejacks, the other hill-toppers made their way cautiously through the slippery snow.

Halfway down the hill, Applejacks broke into a canter. Whitney's grin spread from ear to ear. The pony looked like a snowball rolling down the hill. And the snowball kept gathering speed.

Whitney's grin faded to an O of panic.

"Uh-oh. Runaway pony," Andie said matter-of-factly. In unspoken agreement, Andie and Jina steered their horses into Applejacks's path.

"Whoa! Whoa!" Whitney shouted. But her words flew uselessly into the air.

"Tug hard on your left rein!" Jina instructed, trying to get Whitney to turn the pony in a circle.

But Whitney was grasping the mane with both hands as Applejacks dashed headlong down the hill, charging straight for them. Jina and Andie turned Geoffrey and Ranger sideways so their bodies could be used as a bumper.

"Easy, Geoffrey," Jina crooned, bracing herself. At the last second, the pony ducked his head and slid to a stop. Whitney flew onto his neck, straddled it, then slipped to the ground, landing on her backside with a thump.

For a second, her lower lip quivered as if she were going to cry. Then she sniffed loudly and said, "Gee. That was the first time I ever cantered Apple."

Jina and Andie couldn't help it. They both burst out laughing. By then, Dorothy had ridden up on Windsor.

"Are you all right, Whitney?" she asked worriedly.

The little girl nodded, pouting again. Jina dismounted and grabbed Applejacks's dangling reins. Mary Beth rode up on Dan, followed by Lauren on Whisper. Three other riders trailed behind them.

Whitney got to her feet. When she looked down at her snowy, muddy breeches, her lower lip stuck out even farther. Quickly, Jina reached down and helped brush them off. "Are you sure you're okay?"

Whitney nodded again, then grinned. "Yep. You know what? That was fun!" Taking hold of Apple's bridle, she shook her finger in the pony's face. "Bad boy," she scolded. Then she kissed him on the nose and everybody laughed.

"Well, young lady, I think we'd better take

you back," an older gray-haired woman said. Since she wore hunt colors on her collar, Jina guessed she was the field master for the hill-toppers.

"Already?" Whitney whined. "But I never saw the fox!"

"Sorry," the woman said firmly.

Jina held Applejacks while Whitney scrambled back into the saddle, then she remounted Geoffrey.

"Why aren't you two with the others?" Dorothy asked Jina and Andie.

Andie pointed to Ranger's hind leg. "Wild man here charged into the woods and opened up that old wound. It's stopped bleeding and he isn't lame or anything, but I thought I'd better take him back."

"We're headed that way," the field master said. "I think our hill-toppers are getting cold."

Jina glanced sideways at Lauren and Mary Beth. They both looked tired and wet.

As the group headed back toward Middle-field, Jina steered Geoffrey beside Mary Beth and Lauren. Andie and Ranger had moved to the front with Whitney.

She bit her lip, not sure what to say to her friends. She definitely didn't want to mention the fox. Mary Beth might go into one of her speeches.

And she didn't want to apologize for being such a grump—even though it wasn't all Mary Beth's and Lauren's fault she'd gotten so mad. Still, *she* wasn't the one who had planned the dumb protest. And *So did you have a good time?* seemed too simple after all they'd been through since last night.

Jina sighed and her shoulders slumped. At times like this she wished she were more like her mother. Myra Golden was never at a loss for words.

Beside her, Mary Beth sighed, too. "You know, all the riding around was fun, but I kept hoping I'd actually see a fox."

"You've never seen one?" Jina asked in surprise.

"Only once. In a zoo." Mary Beth shrugged. "It's not the same, though. I wrote that report in fourth grade, so I know all this neat stuff about them, but I've never actually seen one."

"Oh." Again, Jina didn't know what to say. Mary Beth talked about foxes as if they were some rare, exotic animal. Then Jina thought back to the moment she'd spotted the fox weaving through the hedgerow. She had to admit, she'd been pretty excited, too.

"What's that?" Mary Beth suddenly halted Dan.

"What?" Jina and Lauren both looked in every direction.

Mary Beth pointed to the cedar grove. Below the trees was the overgrown stream area where the hounds had lost the fox earlier.

"Look!" Mary Beth said excitedly. "At the edge of the cedars there's something red!"

Lauren arched one brow and looked at Jina.

Mary Beth's arm shook as she jabbed her finger toward the brush. "Right there!" she exclaimed. "See? It's a fox! I finally saw a real fox!"

Jina gazed across the pasture, trying to spot
the fox. Then she looked back at Lauren, confused.

"Do *you* see it?" she whispered.

Lauren shook her head. "No. Hey, wait!
There *is* something moving in and out of the
trees."

"Oh, wow." Mary Beth bounced in the
saddle like a little kid. "A fox. I was afraid
I wouldn't get to see one. I've got to get
closer."

Clucking and kicking, she tried to get Dan
to move away from the other horses. He
wouldn't budge.

"Lauren?" she pleaded. "Will you ride with
me? Just down to the stream?"

Lauren blew out a frosty breath. "I don't

know, Mary Beth. My toes and fingers are numb."

"And we need to ask permission first," Jina added. She nodded toward the field master, who was riding up ahead with the others.

Mary Beth bit her lip. The fox had disappeared. She stared longingly at the cedar trees.

"Okay." Jina gave in. "I'll ride to the stream with you. But only if we get permission."

"All right!" Mary Beth gave her the thumbs-up sign. "Thanks, Jina."

Jina trotted Geoffrey across the pasture. When she told the field master what Mary Beth wanted to do, Dorothy overheard and she chuckled. "Glimpsing Charlie is an experience," she said, using the foxhunter's nickname for the fox.

"I want to see him, too," Whitney insisted.

"No," the field master said quickly. "You older girls may go, but don't stay out long. It's snowing too hard. Do you know the way back?"

Jina nodded. "Middlefield is just over that hill, right?"

"Right. We'll expect you in half an hour."

When Jina trotted back to Mary Beth and Lauren, Ranger and Andie followed.

"You're coming, too?" Jina asked in surprise.

"It's better than riding all the way to Middlefield with Whitney," Andie said. "She's talking my ear off."

When they rode up, Mary Beth gestured for them to hurry. "He's still there!" She pointed in the direction of the cedars.

This time, Jina could see the animal clearly. He was trotting toward the stream, his rusty-red coat making him easy to spot against the white snow.

"Let's follow him," Mary Beth whispered.

"But you saw him already," Lauren protested. Her lips were blue and her earmuffs had slipped sideways. "That's what you wanted, right?"

"I didn't see him up close."

"Come on, guys," Andie said without enthusiasm. "Mary Beth wants to rub noses with the fox. Let's get it over with before we all freeze to death."

Single file, the girls guided their horses down the slippery hill, Jina and Geoffrey leading the way. When they reached the edge of the cedar grove, Jina stopped.

"Look, he must have ducked into that hollow tree," she called, pointing downstream.

"The hounds chased him out of there at the beginning of the hunt."

Mary Beth gasped. "I bet that's his home! How could they chase the poor thing from his own home?"

Andie rolled her eyes. "I knew it. I should have stayed with Whitney. She's not as crazy as you, Finney."

"Laugh all you want, Andie." Mary Beth whirled in the saddle. "I bet *you* wouldn't like to be chased from *your* home."

"Oh, I wouldn't mind as long as I got to take my Renegades tapes," Andie joked. "Besides, how do you know that's his home? Maybe that's where he stashes all the cute bunnies he's going to eat."

"Stop!" Lauren shouted so loudly that Whisper threw her head up. Lauren had dropped her reins so she could plug both ears with her fingers. "Would you two quit it! I'm sick of all this fighting!"

Andie shot Mary Beth a snotty look. "She started it."

"Lauren's right," Jina broke in. "And it's really cold out here. After the hunt, they're having a huge buffet at the master of foxhounds's house. We could get there first."

"Yum." Andie licked her lips. "That sounds good to me."

"Speaking of sounds"—Mary Beth cocked her head—"do you hear that?"

The four girls stopped talking. In the distance, Jina heard the faint singing of the hounds.

"Uh-oh. The hunt's getting closer," she whispered to Andie.

"And they're on the scent of the fox," Andie whispered back.

Jina nodded. She knew exactly what Andie was thinking: *Would Mary Beth do something stupid?*

Turning their heads in unison, they both looked at Mary Beth. Lauren was watching her carefully, too.

Mary Beth chewed the tip of one gloved finger. "Do you think they're on the scent of *our* fox?" she asked worriedly.

Jina opened her mouth to answer, then paused again to listen. The singing of the hounds was getting closer and closer. The pack seemed to be headed straight toward them.

"We'd better get out of here," Andie said, turning Ranger around.

"And leave the fox?" Mary Beth sputtered.

"No way. I vowed to protect him."

"Mary Beth, the fox has eluded the hounds all morning," Jina explained. She glanced anxiously over her shoulder, expecting to see the hounds fly over the crest of the hill any minute. "Don't you think he's smart enough to get away again?"

"No. He's probably tired and hungry and thirsty." Mary Beth put one hand on her hip. "He needs our help. Lauren? Are you coming?"

"What are you going to do?" Lauren asked. She was hunched in her saddle, stiff with cold.

"Chase him off before the hounds get here."

Lauren shook her head weakly. "I can't, Mary Beth. I'm too cold."

"And *I'm* too mature," Andie chimed in. She steered Ranger beside Geoffrey and Whisper so the three horses faced Dan. "Do it yourself, Mary Beth."

Mary Beth stared at her roommates as if she couldn't believe they weren't going to help her. Then she shrugged. "All right. I will do it myself. Come on, Dan."

She pulled hard on the left rein, then slapped him soundly behind the saddle. Startled awake, the big horse jogged a few steps downstream toward the hollow log.

Despite the cold, Jina's palms started to sweat inside her gloves. Behind her, she could hear the hounds, their voices coming closer. It wouldn't be long before the whole pack, huntsman, and whippers-in charged down the hill. And when they did, they'd be furious if they caught them messing with the fox.

"Hurry!" Jina urged.

Mary Beth stopped Dan by the log. Leaning over, she yelled, "Get out of there, fox! Run for your life!"

The fox popped out the other end, and Jina jumped in her saddle, startled. She couldn't believe Mary Beth's idea had worked.

"Shoo! Shoo!" Mary Beth clapped her hands. The fox just stared at her with dull eyes. Jina noticed that his bushy tail drooped. Mary Beth was right—the fox *was* tired.

"Run! Save yourself!" Mary Beth steered Dan toward the fox. Hopping over the stream, the animal disappeared into the thick underbrush on the other side.

Still shouting, Mary Beth kicked and swatted at Dan, trying to get him to follow. Reluctantly, the big horse stepped into the icy water, clambered up the bank, and crashed into the brush after the fox.

The blast of a horn told Jina the huntsman was right behind them. She spun around in her saddle. Beside her, Ranger fidgeted nervously and Whisper pawed the snow.

"We've got to get out of here now," Andie insisted. "Let's trot to the edge of the cedars and look like we're hill-topping."

Jina didn't need to be told twice. She knew the master was already mad at her for bringing two protesters as guests. If he caught them chasing the fox away, he'd kick Jina out of the hunt for sure.

Jina clung to Geoffrey's mane as he charged up the hill after Ranger. Halfway up, she glanced over her shoulder, checking to make sure Lauren and Whisper were behind them. Her friend had been so quiet, Jina was starting to get worried.

When they reached the cedars, they halted their horses side by side. Jina smiled at Lauren between breaths. Her friend gave a shaky smile back. She looked miserably cold. The three girls waited for the hounds to come bounding over the hill. Jina frowned as she listened. Something wasn't right. The hounds' singing was growing fainter, not louder.

"That's weird. Do you think they're on the scent of a different fox?" Andie asked.

"They must be," Jina replied. "They're definitely heading in the other direction."

"You mean they're not coming this way?" Lauren asked. Then before anyone could reply, she burst out laughing. Clutching her stomach, she doubled over so far, the brim of her helmet touched Whisper's mane.

"Let's—not—tell—Mary Beth," she choked out. "She'll—be—so—bummed—she—didn't—save—the—fox."

Andie snorted. "We forgot all about Mary Beth. Do you think we'll find her stuck head-first in some foxhole?"

At that, Jina cracked up, too. Giggling hysterically, the three girls rode back down to the bank of the stream.

"Mary Beth! Come on out wherever you are!" Lauren called. "You saved the fox!" she added, breaking into laughter all over again.

"Do you think our horses will think we lost it?" Jina said between laughs.

"Definitely," Andie gasped. "All they want to do is go home to a nice, dry stall." She peered across the stream. "Where is Mary

Beth, anyway? I'm ready for a nice, dry stall, too." Cupping her hands around her mouth, Andie hollered louder, "Mary Beth!"

"We'd better go find her," Jina said. Picking up her reins, she led the way across the stream.

Behind her, Lauren sighed wearily. "At least she'll be easy to follow. Dan's hoofprints are the size of plates."

"*Plates*." Andie groaned. "Don't say that word. It reminds me of food."

"You mean like roast beef, ham, fruit salad, steamed shrimp, and veggie dip?" Jina said. "All the delicious things the hunt's having at the buffet?"

Andie groaned again. "Cut it out. Come on, let's hurry and find Finney so we can get back quick."

But ten minutes later, they hadn't found Mary Beth. Dan's trail wound deeper and deeper into the woods, and when the girls called, there was no reply.

"Where could she have gone?" Andie called up to Jina. She and Ranger were behind Lauren and Whisper. "Florida?"

"She must still be following that fox," Jina

called back. "She's crazy!"

"I'm cold," Lauren complained tiredly. "And my nose won't stop running."

"Well, my butt's gone to sleep," Andie grumbled. "And my toes must be frostbitten because I can't feel them anymore."

Jina held up one hand. "Hey, I think I hear something." She nudged Geoffrey with her heels. He plunged under some low-hanging branches and into a small clearing.

Immediately, she spotted Dan's broad backside. He was standing still, but there was no rider on him.

Then a movement on the ground made Jina draw in her breath. Mary Beth was lying in the snow in front of Dan. She was flat on her back, thrashing wildly, her arms and legs at odd angles.

"It's Mary Beth!" Jina cried in alarm. "And something's horribly wrong!"

10

"Mary Beth!" Jina called. She jumped off Geoffrey and raced to her friend's side. *Had she fallen off? Was she wild with pain?*

Kneeling, Jina grasped Mary Beth's wrist. Her skin felt cold and damp. Jina's mind whirled, trying to remember back to health class. What did you do for someone suffering from—what was it called?— hypothermia?

"Mary Beth!" she repeated urgently, trying not to sound too hysterical.

Mary Beth quit thrashing and raised her head. "What?" she asked impatiently.

Jina's eyes widened at the sudden change in her roommate. "Are you all right?"

"I'm fine." Sitting up, Mary Beth unsnapped her helmet and took it off. "Just a little wet," she said, dusting the snow off the velvet.

By then, Lauren and Andie had ridden into the clearing. Lauren jumped off Whisper and grabbed Geoffrey's loose reins.

"What's wrong? Why are you on the ground like that? Did Dan throw you?" Lauren asked in a rush.

Mary Beth frowned. "Throw me? *Dan?*" She glanced over at her horse and giggled. He'd ambled over to a bush and was picking around at the dry leaves. A piece of honeysuckle vine hung from his mouth. "No way."

"Then what's going on?" Andie demanded. She was still mounted on Ranger. Tugging on the reins, he tried to snatch a leaf, too. "Jina thought something was wrong. Though everything seems okay to me." She gave Jina an accusing look.

"Well, I—I—" Jina stammered as she glanced from Lauren to Andie. Her gaze settled on Mary Beth, who really did look okay now. "She was rolling around in the snow," she explained. "I *thought* she was hurt."

"Hurt?" Mary Beth put her helmet back on her head. "I was only trying to erase the fox's prints." She pointed to the giant snow angel she had made with her body.

"I'm messing up his scent, too," she continued. "The hounds will come running into the clearing, smell me in this spot, and be totally confused. That will give the fox tons of time to get away." She smiled triumphantly at her three roommates.

Jina stood up. "They aren't the only ones who are totally confused," she murmured, shaking her head.

Andie burst out laughing. "Only you would do something like that, Finney. You are such a—"

"Brilliant roommate," Lauren broke in, glaring at Andie. "Thanks to you, the hounds will *never* catch that fox. Now, *let's go back to Middlefield!*" she ended with a shout.

Mary Beth jerked up her chin. "What's wrong with her?" she asked Jina, frowning.

"Lauren's just cold," Jina explained as she took Geoffrey's reins. She didn't want to mention to Mary Beth that the hounds weren't even heading in this direction.

"Cold? Then let's do some calisthenics before we mount up," Mary Beth suggested enthusiastically. She got up and, raising her arms, started doing jumping jacks. "One, two, three—"

Andie put her hand to the side of her

mouth. "Do you think she's suffering from overexposure?" she whispered to Jina and Lauren.

"Probably, except she's right. A little exercise *will* warm us up." Still holding Geoffrey's reins, Jina started doing jumping jacks, too. With a sigh, Lauren joined them.

Grumbling loudly, Andie dismounted and did a halfhearted jump. "I hate exercise. Why don't we pretend we're sunbathing at the beach instead?"

After reaching twenty, Mary Beth stopped jumping. "There!" She beamed at her roommates. "Now isn't that better?"

Lauren cocked her head. "Actually, I do feel a little warmer," she admitted.

"Me too. Except for the tingle in my toes." Andie frowned down at her boots. "I hope that means I'm getting feeling back in them."

"I think it means they're about to fall off," Jina said seriously.

Andie's brows shot up. "What?" When Jina started to laugh, Andie's dark eyes narrowed. Reaching down, she picked up a handful of snow and began packing it. "Start running, Williams," she warned.

Still laughing, Jina darted around Geoffrey.

The snowball flew through the air, hitting Dan's rump with a solid whack. He paused for just a second, then reached into the tangle of honeysuckle for another bite.

"All right, children," Lauren said. "Quit fighting. The field master said we had to hurry back."

Andie nodded vigorously. "Right. For the *buffet*," she said, smacking her lips.

"Mmm." Mary Beth patted her own stomach. "All that fox saving has made me hungry."

"Well, you guys are in luck," Jina said, walking around to the back of her saddle where her nylon saddlebags hung from the rings. Unbuckling the flap, she pulled out four granola bars. "Maybe these will help."

She passed out the snacks, and for a few minutes, the girls munched in silence. Jina checked her watch. It was almost noon. When she looked up at the treetops, a flurry of snowflakes pelted her in the face. It was snowing harder.

"We'd better get back," Jina said, stuffing the last bite into her mouth. "Don't forget to put your trash in your pocket."

"Will you give me a leg up?" Lauren asked her.

"Me too," Mary Beth said.

"And me!" Andie demanded.

When everyone was mounted, Jina steered Geoffrey back the way they had come. She kept her eyes trained on the trail as he picked his way around the trees and brush.

This time, she didn't feel like poking along admiring the winter scenery. She was too cold and hungry. The granola bar had only made her stomach growl louder.

"I'm glad you know the way," Mary Beth said behind her. "I didn't realize how far into the woods that fox led me."

"I don't really know the way," Jina admitted. "But we left a trail a mile wide in the snow."

"Well, we'd better hurry up." Lauren called. "The snow is already covering up our tracks. Except where we were snacking and exercising." She and Whisper were following behind Dan.

Ten minutes later, they reached the stream. Jina halted Geoffrey and peered right, then left. A confusion of prints led over the rushing water in several places. In front of her, the bank dipped sharply into the water. *Where was the spot they had crossed?*

"Great," Jina muttered under her breath.

Mary Beth rode Dan up beside Geoffrey. "What's wrong?"

"There are so many hoofprints, I'm not sure which ones are ours," Jina told her.

"Who else's would they be?"

"The huntsman's or the whippers-in's. They were charging around here earlier."

"What's the problem?" Lauren asked. She and Andie had halted their horses behind Geoffrey and Dan.

"She doesn't know where to cross," Mary Beth called over her shoulder.

"Just cross anywhere," Andie said impatiently. "The pasture's got to be on the other side. Somewhere."

Jina peered across the stream. For some reason, it didn't look familiar. The woods were too dark and overgrown. Wasn't the pasture supposed to be on the other side of the stream? *This had to be right*, she told herself.

Guiding Geoffrey upstream, she found an easier place to cross. Still, the horses slid down the snowy bank. Ranger, the last to cross, hesitated on the edge.

"Uh-oh, he's going to jump," Andie said. "Whoa, Ranger. Whoa." Sitting deep, she tightened her reins, but it didn't do any good.

Bunching into a tight ball, Ranger leaped across the water. Andie grabbed mane, but still she got left behind. She hit the saddle hard.

"All right?" Jina asked.

Andie nodded, wincing. Ranger pranced a few steps, then settled in behind Whisper. Jina scanned the ground, hunting again for their trail. "Does anyone see our tracks?"

"There!" Lauren pointed to a trail leading away from the stream.

The tracks were covered with snow, but Jina could make out blurred hoofprints. She followed them with her gaze. "It seems as if they're leading in the right direction."

She urged Geoffrey forward. A clump of snow fell from a tree limb, landing with a plop in front of him. Jina clenched and unclenched her fingers, trying to warm them. The cold had crept down her neck and up her sleeves, numbing her bare skin.

Fifteen minutes later, Jina halted Geoffrey, and frowned, staring ahead. The trail they were following doubled back. And ahead of them was deep woods. The pasture that was supposed to be on the other side of the stream was nowhere in sight.

Jina felt a sinking feeling deep in her stomach. She twisted in the saddle. Lauren, Mary Beth, and Andie were silently watching her. "Are we almost there?" Mary Beth asked hopefully.

Jina took a deep breath. "Uh, not really. In fact, I have some bad news." She bit her lip, then blurted, "I think we're lost!"

"Ha, ha, ha! Pretty funny, Jina," Andie said. "I'd laugh harder except my lips are frozen shut. Now quit joking and get us out of here."

Tears pricked Jina's eyes. "I'm not joking. I really don't know where we are."

"You don't?" Lauren and Mary Beth chorused.

"You mean we're really lost?" Andie stared at her in disbelief.

Sniffling softly, Jina nodded. "I'm sorry, guys. Sorry for everything." Tears spilled from her eyes, running down her cheeks in two cold streams. "I wanted these two days to be *perfect*. Only the sleep over was a bomb and so was the protest and now we're lost and—"

And you all had a lousy time, and you probably don't want to be my friends anymore.

Andie glared at her. "Why are *you* apologizing, Jina?" Turning, she pointed an accusing finger at Mary Beth. "It's all Finney's fault. First *she* ruined your sleep over, then *she* almost got us kicked out of the hunt, now *she* chases some fox into the woods and gets us all lost."

Mary Beth's lower lip started to quiver. "But I only wanted to—to—save—the—fox," she said in a trembling voice.

"Okay, okay," Lauren soothed. "Crying's not going to help us find our way back to Middlefield."

Steering Whisper next to Dan, Lauren stood in her stirrups and patted Mary Beth's shoulder. Then she rode over to Geoffrey and patted Jina's arm, trying to make her feel better, too.

But Jina didn't feel better. She was too cold and lost and miserable.

Just then, Geoffrey threw up his head and Ranger snorted. Startled, Whisper wheeled around, and even Dan pricked up his ears.

"What are they looking at?" Andie whispered.

Jina shook her head. "I don't know. Wait, look!" She pointed to the bank of the stream. About fifty feet away, a streak of red darted among the exposed tree roots.

"It's the fox!" Mary Beth breathed.

Lauren's mouth fell open. "Do you think it's the one you saved, Mary Beth?"

Mary Beth shrugged. "I don't know." Silently, they all watched the fox until it disappeared.

Jina glanced over her shoulder at Mary Beth. "You know, Mary Beth, the protest was sort of dumb, but I think I understand why you and Lauren did it."

Mary Beth looked surprised.

"You do?"

"Yeah." Jina wiped the last tear from her cheek. "They're really beautiful animals. And they certainly belong out here more than we do."

"I guess you're right, Williams," Andie agreed reluctantly. "Not that you'll ever catch *me* waving some stupid poster around."

"Oh, good." Lauren looked relieved. "I'm glad everybody made up. Now can we go home? I'm soooo cold and hungry."

"Sure," Andie said. "As soon as someone figures out the way."

And I guess that someone is supposed to be me, Jina thought glumly. Brushing snowflakes from her lashes, she gazed into the woods, hoping to recognize a tree or bush or *something*.

"Well, Jina?" Andie prompted. "Are you waiting for a sign that says this way?"

Lauren stuck her lip out. "I guess we really are lost. That means I'll never see Todd again."

"I thought it was his younger brother you were in love with," Mary Beth said. "Spencer, right?"

"No, Andie loves Spencer."

"I do not. He's just cute, that's all. Hey, Jina, why wasn't he foxhunting today?" Andie asked.

Jina only half heard the question. She was still trying to figure out how to get out of this mess. "Jina?"

"Hmmm?"

"Will you get with it, Williams?" Andie demanded. "We're discussing important things here. Lauren wanted to know why Spencer isn't at the hunt."

"I did not," Lauren fumed. "*You* did."

Jina could only stare at her roommates in disbelief. All three were soaking wet and blue with cold. How could they even think about boys at a time like this?

"I don't know why he's not hunting today,"

Jina said impatiently. "And I don't care. I'm trying to figure out how to get us all out of here."

"Haven't you hunted at Middlefield a zillion times before?" Mary Beth asked.

Jina shook her head. "Just a couple of times last year. It wasn't snowing then, and I don't remember this part of the woods at all." She fell into a gloomy silence.

Beside her, Ranger pawed the snow impatiently, Whisper chewed her bit, and Dan jerked the reins from Mary Beth's grasp so he could reach a brown leaf. Even the ever-patient Geoffrey shook his head.

Jina reached down to give him a pat. "Geoffrey here is the only who's hunted all..." She stopped abruptly as an idea came to her. "That's it!"

Lauren whirled in her saddle to look at her. "What's it?"

"Geoffrey can get us out of here," Jina said excitedly.

Andie slapped her cheek. "What a good idea!" she said. "I bet he even has a map in his pocket."

Jina turned to face Andie. "He doesn't need a map. I bet he probably knew how to get home all along."

"Jina's right," Lauren chimed in, nodding. "I read an article about trail riding at night. Horses can see and smell much better than humans. So even if Geoffrey doesn't know which way is home, he can probably smell our old trail."

Mary Beth tugged on Dan's reins, trying to get him to pick up his head. "Let's go for it. Pretty soon, I'm going to be so hungry I'll join Dan in a lunch of leaves."

"I guess we've got nothing to lose." Bending over Ranger's neck, Andie shook her finger at Geoffrey. "All right, horse, find the shrimp and roast beef."

Jina laughed. "That's not going to do it." Aiming Geoffrey toward the woods, she slackened the reins and squeezed lightly with her legs. "Geoffrey, find your sweetfeed and stablemates."

Instantly, Geoffrey headed off into the trees at a determined pace. Lauren steered Whisper right behind him.

"Do you really think he knows where he's going?" Lauren whispered to Jina.

"We'll soon find out—oops, *watch the branch!*" she added suddenly, ducking to avoid getting smacked in the face.

Geoffrey lowered his head and blew noisily as he picked his way around trees, brambles, and fallen logs. Jina held her breath every time he swerved, hoping they were going in the right direction.

"Is this the scenic route?" Andie called to the front. Jina had to chuckle as she shook her head. Even when things were really bad, Andie could always crack a joke.

Ten minutes later, they came to a stream.

"What? I can't believe it!" Jina pulled back on the reins. "We crossed this stream already!" She groaned as she looked back at the others. Geoffrey must have taken them in a circle!

"Well, so much for horse sense," Andie muttered as she halted Ranger behind her.

"Wait a minute." Mary Beth pointed across the stream. "Look! We weren't going in circles. There's the pasture. And the hollow log. It must have been a different stream we crossed earlier. That's why it didn't look familiar."

Jina squinted. Beyond the trees and brush, she glimpsed gray sky and snow-covered grass. "Mary Beth's right!" she said, grinning excitedly at her roommates. "We made it, guys! We really made it!"

12

"You mean we're *un*lost!" Lauren gave a whoop of joy, and Mary Beth and Andie cheered and clapped.

Jina fell onto Geoffrey's wet mane. "Thank you, thank you for getting us out of there," she whispered, giving him a hug.

When she looked up, Lauren and Whisper were sloshing through the stream. Andie and Ranger had already bounded across and out of the wooded area. Mary Beth flashed Jina a hesitant smile. "Hey, Jina, I knew all the time you'd get us home," she said as she steered Dan across the stream. "You're the roommate we can always count on."

"Uh, thanks," Jina replied. She wasn't sure if that was a compliment or not.

Geoffrey twisted one ear, waiting for a signal. Grabbing mane, Jina gave him his head. By now she knew she could trust him to get her safely across the stream—and home.

That must be what Mary Beth meant, Jina thought. She was a bit like Geoffrey. Dependable and sensible. A friend you could count on.

And that was okay, Jina decided. Sure, she'd rather be charming and witty like her famous-star mom. Or feisty and funny like Andie, or sweet and cute like Lauren, or determined and outgoing like Mary Beth.

But she wasn't any of those things. She was just herself.

"Middlefield looks deserted," Lauren said as the girls rode their horses side by side up the last hill. They had passed through the gate next to the log fence and were walking through the pasture behind Middlefield's barn.

Lauren's right, Jina realized as she looked around. The place was dead quiet—no hounds, horses, or people trotting back and forth.

"Do you think everybody went looking for us?" Mary Beth asked, sounding worried. "You know, like a search party?"

Jina shrugged. "We're not that late. But

maybe they were concerned about us since it's so cold."

"Concerned? Ha!" Andie pointed to the gravel parking lot at one end of the barn. Most of the trailers were gone, and in the distance, a van was rumbling down the drive to the paved road.

"Everybody rushed home to change for the brunch," Andie continued. "I bet they're going to beat us to all that shrimp!"

Mary Beth snorted. "Well, that's real nice. What if we really had gotten lost? No one would have even noticed!"

"Someone would have noticed *eventually*," Jina assured Mary Beth, though she wasn't so sure herself. Even the limo was gone.

She glanced over at her friends. They were mud splattered and wet from head to hoof. Mary Beth's earmuffs were cockeyed, Andie's damp hair straggled from under her helmet, and Lauren's lips were cracked.

Jina's shoulders slumped wearily. She could tell from her roommates' expressions that they'd had a terrible time.

Not that she blamed them.

When they reached the gate leading to the drive, Andie and Ranger led the way. As Jina brought up the rear, Dorothy charged around the corner of the barn. She'd taken off her riding boots and hunt coat and thrown on warmer gear.

"Would you girls quit fooling around and get in here?" Dorothy scolded. "The field was back an hour ago. And look at your horses!" She clucked her tongue in disapproval. "Their legs are covered with mud. You need to get them cleaned off so we can go eat."

Andie smirked at the others. "See? I told you. No one even noticed."

"Noticed what?" Dorothy grabbed hold of Dan's bridle so Mary Beth could dismount. When she slid from the saddle, her knees buckled.

"Ouch," she said, grabbing the stirrup leather for support. "I'll never walk again."

Dorothy continued to fuss like a mother hen. "You'd better, because Dan is going to need lots of cooling off. That goes for all of you—up and down the aisle until those horses are dry."

Mary Beth groaned again, and Lauren and Andie grimaced tiredly. With a sigh, Jina dismounted. Her toes were so cold she couldn't feel them.

Dorothy waved them into the barn. Leading Geoffrey, Jina hobbled after her. Her boots had rubbed a raw spot by her knee and her legs felt like rubber.

"Middlefield's letting us borrow stalls for Whisper, Dan, and Ranger," Dorothy said as the girls followed her down the aisle. She stopped opposite three empty stalls. The Foxhall horses' coolers, halters, blankets, and grooming buckets were already waiting. "We'll van them home after the buffet."

"Buffet?" Andie croaked, propping herself against Ranger's neck. "Do you think there'll be any food left by the time we get there?"

"Not if you don't get moving," Dorothy said briskly. She bustled back and forth, helping the girls untack their horses.

Jina led Geoffrey down the aisle to his stall. "You definitely deserve a rubdown," she told him as she took off his bridle and put on his halter. Looping the bridle over her shoulder, she hooked him to crossties.

Steam rose from his back, and he was soaking wet. Jina was exhausted, but she knew Dorothy was right. None of them could sit down until their horses were cool.

Jina hung Geoffrey's bridle on the hook

outside his stall. Andie had thrown a wool cooler on Ranger and was walking toward her up the aisle. Her helmet strap was unsnapped and she scuffed her boots on the concrete.

"I bet everyone is eating right now," Andie grumbled as she turned Ranger back to walk the way they had come.

With a sigh, Jina didn't answer. Instead, she slid her saddle off and propped it up against the wall. She couldn't blame Andie—or Lauren or Mary Beth—for grumbling. The whole two days had been one big disaster.

Tears pricked Jina's eyes. *I'm not very good at this friendship thing*, she thought. But then she'd never had much practice. She'd gone to too many different schools and spent too much time showing Superstar. It was no wonder she was a friendship failure.

Twenty minutes later, Jina had rubbed and walked Geoffrey until he was almost dry. She hooked him to the crossties, took a dandy brush from his grooming bucket, and swiped at the mud on his legs.

"Almost ready?" Lauren asked, coming up behind her.

Jina nodded. "I just have to get this mud out of his tail."

"Yeah. Whisper's was a mess, too." Lauren leaned back against the wall. Jina noticed she'd taken off her boots and put on tennis shoes. Jina thought about the sweater and skirt she'd brought to wear to the buffet.

"Are you going to change clothes before eating?" Jina asked.

Lauren shook her head. "No. Andie's already chomping at the bit to hit the food line. Dorothy said she'd drive us over " She hesitated. "Jina, I want to apologize—"

Just then, Dorothy swung open the tack room door. "Are you girls ready?"

"Yes!" Lauren jumped away from the wall. "Andie and Mary Beth are putting away their grooming buckets."

"Geoffrey's ready, too," Jina replied. *What had Lauren been about to apologize for?* she wondered. She, Jina, was the only one who should be sorry for anything.

Unhooking the crossties, Jina led Geoffrey into his stall. He ducked his head and grabbed a huge mouthful of hay.

"You're a pig!" Jina laughed at the wad falling from his mouth. But she had a feeling that was exactly how *she* was going to look at the buffet table.

Ten minutes later, the girls were squished into the front cab of the Foxhall pickup truck. They rode down the drive in silence. Jina had taken off her boots and hunt coat and changed into tennis shoes and a sweater. She felt better already.

"I smell onion dip," Andie said, glancing accusingly at Dorothy.

The older woman grinned. "It was good, too. Hey, Jina, your mom was looking for you. I told her I was picking you up, and you'd be at Mr. Brink's house any minute."

"My mom came?" Jina said in surprise.

"Yes. She brought your grandmother, too."

"That's neat," Mary Beth commented.

"I guess." Jina gazed out the window. Her mother was usually at the studio on Saturday mornings.

So why had she driven all the way out to Middlefield? Maybe it had something to do with the protest, she decided. Maybe she was going to interview Mary Beth and Lauren.

"And your dad's there, Andie," Dorothy said.

"My *dad*!" Andie exclaimed so loudly that the barn manager winced.

"I believe he said it was easier to pick you up here than drive into Baltimore. Jina's grandmother brought your things."

"Oh?" Andie said, softer this time.

At least her dad's there because of her, Jina thought a little bitterly. *Not because of a stupid TV show.*

There were dozens of cars parked in front of Mr. Brink's home, a colonial-style mansion with white columns and shutters. A shrub-lined walkway led to the front steps, and two narrow pines flanked the steps like guards.

Dorothy parked behind a silver Mercedes. Two cars ahead, Jina could see the limo. She pictured Charles sitting inside, listening to a CD and doing a crossword.

"I sent Charles over here earlier," Dorothy told Jina. "He looked hungry and cold so I told him to get some grub."

"Thanks."

"Nice place," Andie commented as she climbed out of the truck.

"It's about a hundred years old," Jina said. "Mr. and Mrs. Brink restored it."

Mary Beth sniffed the air. "Is that food I

smell? Or is my nose playing tricks on me?"

"Yes! Yes!" Andie threw her arms wide as she raced up the snowy walk. Mary Beth, Lauren, and Jina were right behind her.

"Here I come, roast beef! Here I come, chips and dip!" Andie sang out. Leaping up the steps, she lunged against the door.

"Go on in," Dorothy called, laughing, "before you eat the paint off."

The four girls crowded into the dark foyer. Mrs. Brink, a short, round woman wearing a white blouse and a tartan kilt, bustled over to greet them.

"You girls must be starved," she said. "Take off your wet shoes, then go right into the dining room." She waved down the hall. "There's still plenty to eat."

"Jina! Andie! Mary Beth! Lauren!" Whitney, wearing a navy velvet party dress, burst into the foyer and threw herself into Jina's arms. Just as quickly, she popped back.

"Come on, hurry!" she urged. Grabbing Jina's hand, then Lauren's, Whitney began to drag the two girls into a room right off the hall.

"Wait, Whitney!" Jina protested. "We want to eat first. We're starving."

"There's no time!" Whitney jerked impatiently on Jina's hand. "You have to come, all of you. We're going to be on TV!"

13

"We really made the news?" Mary Beth exclaimed.

Jina's heart sank.

Whitney nodded excitedly. "Yes! Jina's mom just called the TV station to check. We're going to be on the weekend news. And that's right now!"

Lauren and Mary Beth exchanged big grins. Bending, they hurried to take off their wet shoes.

"Wow," Lauren gasped as she hopped on one foot. "I can't believe it. Our protest made the news!"

"Come on." Whitney dropped Jina's hand and grabbed Mary Beth's. "Let's go. There's a TV in the den."

Andie rolled her eyes, then nudged Jina

with her elbow. "What do you think? Should we go watch the stars? Or eat?"

"I'm going to eat. But you should go watch, Andie. You and Ranger were there. Maybe the cameraman got a shot of you."

Andie brightened. "True. This might be my big break. I could be discovered by an agent looking for the next Miss Teen America."

"Yeah, sure." Jina bit back a grin. She wondered if Andie knew how bedraggled she looked, with mud streaking her cheeks and her thick, curly hair sticking out every which way.

"You just wait. And when I'm famous, I'll finally make enough money to buy Magic." Andie twirled like a ballerina and, tossing a smile over her shoulder, ran to join the others in the den.

As soon as Andie was gone, Jina's own smile faded. Slowly, she trudged down the hall in her socks to the dining room. The buffet table looked like an army had tromped through it. Food was strewn everywhere. But Jina didn't care. There was plenty left to eat.

Her mouth watered as she piled her plate with fruit, cheese, crackers, ham slices, dip, rolls, and salads. She stuck a napkin and fork in the pocket of her breeches, grabbed a glass of punch, and headed into the living room.

It was empty except for a few grown-ups she didn't recognize. *Where is everyone?* she wondered.

Perching on the end of an antique sofa, Jina pulled her fork from her pocket and began to eat. She stuffed a strawberry in her mouth, then took a big bite of ham. The blaring music from the TV, followed by sounds of laughter, made her stop in mid-chew.

So that's where everybody is, Jina realized. Her friends, her mother, grandmother, Mrs. Caufield, Dorothy, Todd, even Mr. Brink were in the den watching the big news.

"We're on next!" Jina heard Whitney squeal above the noise.

Jina gulped down the ham. The handful of people who had been sipping punch left the living room, too.

Jina had never felt more alone.

With a sigh, she took another bite. At least her mother could have come in to say hello, she thought.

Oh, stop being such a baby, she scolded herself. *By now you should be used to sharing your mother with an audience.*

"Hello, Jina," a voice greeted her in a soft

drawl. Jina looked up. Her grandmother was standing in the doorway, dressed in a dark blue dress with a high, lacy collar. And as usual whenever she went out, she was wearing her favorite string of pearls.

"Oh, Grandma."

Grandmother Williams shuffled into the room and, using the sofa arm for support, lowered herself next to Jina. "What you doing here all alone, child?"

Placing one finger under Jina's chin, she tilted her granddaughter's face toward her. "Ah, is that sadness I see in your pretty golden eyes?"

"No," Jina said, jerking away from her. "I'm just tired, that's all."

Her grandmother laughed gently. "Tired, yes. Alone, yes. Why? Because of your friends? Did you have a misunderstanding?"

Jina shook her head. Angrily, she stabbed a strawberry with her fork. *Go away, Grandma.*

Her grandmother leaned back with a sigh. "Ahhhh. I remember when I was your age."

Jina concentrated on her plate.

"My friend Evelyn and I bickered constantly. Only back then, we lived on Charles Street in Baltimore. In a tiny row house, not a fancy condo on the water. I should take you there someday, Jinaki."

Jina peeked over at her grandmother. She was plucking at the folds of her skirt. Eyes bright, she stared straight ahead as if lost in thought.

"That was so many years ago. Still, we fought about the same things you and your friends probably fight about. Hurt feelings and jealousies. My father worked hard, so I seldom saw him. One night, he came home, pale and weary. Evelyn and I were sitting on the stoop. I rushed to greet him. But when he hugged me, his eyes were on Evelyn. She'd gotten a new dress." Her grandmother paused, and Jina noticed how her head shook slightly.

"I was crushed," her grandmother whispered, her voice quivering. "I didn't speak to Evelyn for weeks. I thought my father was paying more attention to her than me. Actually, he was just feeling bad because he couldn't buy me a new dress, too."

Jina set her plate on her knees and slid her fingers around her grandmother's gnarled ones. "Did you and Evelyn ever make up?"

Her grandmother smiled faintly. "Oh, yes.

Last year she died in a nursing home. We were still writing to each other." She gave Jina's fingers a reassuring squeeze. "So you see, Jinaki, friendship is never easy."

Jina nodded. She did understand. "Come on, Grandma," she said, putting her plate on an end table. "Let's go into the den. We can watch the news together."

Jina helped Grandma Williams up and, holding her hand, guided her into the den. It was packed with people.

Her mother sat on a couch in front of the TV with Lauren and Mary Beth on either side of her. Whitney cuddled back on her lap, and Andie was sitting on the floor by her knees. When Myra saw Jina and Grandma Williams, she waved them over.

Jina steered her grandmother through the crowd. Andie's father, Mr. Perez, stood off by himself in a corner, his back ramrod straight. With his polished loafers, button-down shirt collar, and serious expression, he seemed out of place among the rumpled riders.

"The news anchor just announced us," Mary Beth whispered as Jina came up behind the couch. Her green eyes were wide as saucers. "'Protest at Middlefield.' We're going to be on after this commercial."

"Can you believe it?" Lauren mumbled. She was nervously chewing her nails. "Thanks to your mom, we're going to be on TV!"

Thanks to your mom. Jina felt a familiar stab of anger at her roommate's words. But then she quickly brushed it aside. *Friendship is never easy,* she reminded herself.

Abruptly, Mary Beth jumped up from the couch. "Here it comes! Here it comes!" she cried, pointing to the TV.

"Shhhh!" Whitney hushed loudly. Embarrassed, Mary Beth sat down again.

The newscaster was introducing the next segment. A picture of Middlefield flashed on the TV, and everyone in the room cheered. Next, the camera swung to the huntsman and the hounds, and panned over the field of riders.

Then Mr. Brink galloped into view, and the camera zoomed in on his red face and scowling eyes. Jina peered cautiously over her shoulder at the real Mr. Brink. He was laughing and talking as he gestured toward the TV.

"This will be good publicity for the hunt," he was telling the man beside him.

Jina was surprised by the master's reaction. He didn't seem mad at all about the protest now.

She turned her attention back to the TV. There was so much talking and laughing in the room, she could barely hear what the newscaster was saying. Andie scooted forward to turn up the volume just as the picture switched to Whitney, who was dancing around waving her poster.

"There's me!" Whitney squealed.

"Shhh!" Andie said.

A hush fell over the room as everyone focused on the screen. Even Jina held her breath.

"Can the sport of foxhunting survive local animal rights protests?" the announcer said. "At Middlefield Stables today two sixth-grade Foxhall Academy students…"

This is their big moment, Jina thought, suddenly growing excited as a shot of Lauren and Mary Beth, holding their posters, flashed on the screen. Then her mouth fell open in surprise. The cameraman had cut off her roommates' heads!

14

"And that's the news for today," the announcer finished. "Stay tuned for..."

"That's *it?*" Mary Beth croaked.

All around Jina, groups of people were laughing and talking as they drifted from the den. Mary Beth, Lauren, and Andie hadn't taken their eyes off the TV.

Whitney sprang off Myra's lap. "Oh, I was so cute!" She whirled in a circle. "I've got to find Todd and tell him all about it."

She danced from the room, bumping into people as she went. Standing up, Myra went over and switched off the TV. Mary Beth, Andie, and Lauren still hadn't moved.

"Well, girls, that was quite something wasn't it?" Myra asked. Jina noticed her mother was wearing a stylish suede jacket over a long gathered skirt. Suede boots and dangly turquoise earrings complemented the outfit.

She must be going to the studio after this, Jina thought with a sigh.

Grandma Williams shuffled around the sofa to sit next to Mary Beth. "Your posters were lovely, dear," she said, patting her hand.

"But they cut off my head," Mary Beth protested.

"And all anyone saw was Ranger's legs!" Andie wailed. "And one boot! They didn't get my face at all!"

Disappointed, Lauren shook her head. "I called my parents to tell them to watch. But I bet they won't even know it was me."

Mary Beth sighed. "All that work for nothing."

"Now, now. You girls weren't protesting just to get on TV. Am I correct?" Myra asked. Hands on her hips, she questioned the group as if they were guests on her talk show.

Mary Beth and Lauren nodded reluctantly, their eyes focused on Jina's mother. Even Jina watched her in fascination. Myra Golden spoke with such assurance and moved with such grace that she demanded people's attention.

"You were protesting to save the fox," Myra reminded them. "Right?"

The girls nodded again, sheepishly this time. Jina noticed that Andie's father had joined the group. He stood behind Andie, who was sitting on the sofa, and placed one hand on her shoulder.

"So it was all worthwhile," Myra finished with a nod.

"Ms. Golden's right," Mr. Perez said, patting Andie awkwardly.

Andie snorted. "It was supposed to be my ticket to fame and fortune. I figured agents would be calling to ask me to be the next National Velvet."

Jina clapped a hand over her mouth to hold back a giggle. Mary Beth and Lauren laughed out loud. Even Mr. Perez cracked a smile.

"I didn't realize being a movie star was going to be your ticket to fame," Mr. Perez commented.

Andie looked at him suspiciously. "What do you mean?"

"Aren't you the young lady who started her own business at Foxhall?" he reminded her.

Myra chuckled. "Jina told me all about it. The girls made quite a bit of money."

"A hundred dollars. And it was all my daughter's idea," Mr. Perez said proudly.

Not all her idea, Jina wanted to say, but she bit her tongue. Andie had flushed bright red at her father's compliment. Jina knew how much it meant to her friend.

"Well, yeah. Except the dean made us give the money back," Andie grumbled. She peered up at her father. "Hey, do you think there's any other way I can make enough money to buy Magic?"

At that, everybody started laughing again. They all knew Andie would never give up.

Mr. Perez smiled. "I'll think about it."

Jina's mom went over and linked her arm through his. "Well, Mr. Perez, how would like a tour of the Brinks' home before you leave? It's on the county's historical register."

He raised one brow. "Really? I'd like that."

"Mother? Would you like to come too?" Myra turned to Grandma Williams. The older woman nodded and Jina helped her off the couch.

"Uh, Mom, are you working today?" Jina asked in a low voice.

Her mother shook her head. "Why, no, honey, I'm spending the afternoon with my two favorite people," she said, kissing Jina's brow. "My favorite daughter and my favorite mother."

Jina felt a huge weight lift off her shoulders. She watched happily as Myra, Grandma Williams, and Mr. Perez left the room.

"Did you hear that?" Andie reached over and slapped her on the knee. "My father said he'll think about it! That means he hasn't totally ruled out buying Magic."

"Maybe he'll buy him for you for Christmas," Lauren said.

"Christmas! Wow, I never thought about that." Andie slumped back against the sofa, a glazed look in her eyes.

Jina sat on the edge of the sofa, thinking.

At the beginning of the school year, she had tried to keep to herself. The old Jina was used to studying and riding hard and minding her own business.

But that hadn't worked at Foxhall. Andie, Lauren, and Mary Beth had pulled her into their squabbles and adventures. Now Jina realized that, no matter how nerve-racking these past two days had been, she could never go back to being the old Jina. And she didn't want to, either.

Just then Mary Beth's stomach rumbled, breaking the silence. She slapped her hand over it. "Time to eat," she announced.

"Wait!" Lauren jumped up. Nervously, she wound her fingers together. "I think we ought to apologize to Jina first."

Mary Beth looked as puzzled as Jina.

Lauren took a deep breath. "If we were going to protest, we should have picked a different foxhunt. It wasn't fair to you, Jina. We could have gotten you in big trouble."

"Lauren's right," Mary Beth agreed slowly, glancing down at her hands clasped between her knees. "It was pretty rude and selfish of me to ruin the sleep over and the hunt for you just because of a fox."

"Yeah, Finney, you were a knucklehead," Andie said. "And you, Williams"—she whacked Jina with a throw pillow—"were a pretty good sport."

Now it was Jina's turn to flush. If only they knew what a bad sport she'd been inside.

"You guys don't need to apologize," she mumbled. "*I'm* the one who should apologize. I know none of you had much fun—"

"Hey, I had a blast," Andie cut in. "The last hunt I went on was bor-r-ring. We sat around all morning waiting for a stupid fox to show up, and he never did."

"I had a great time, too!" Mary Beth insisted. "My brothers and sister will be so excited when I tell them about scaring the fox and chasing him into the woods."

Lauren nodded. "Me too. And I'd love to come back and visit you in Baltimore again, Jina. It was so cool. Only next time you have to take us all around Harborplace."

Jina stared at her roommates. She couldn't believe it. They really had had a good time!

Jina grinned from ear to ear. "Well, I had a super time, too. And you know why? Because my three best friends were there."

Jumping off the sofa, Mary Beth raised her fist in the air. "Three cheers for the best sleep over ever!"

"Hip, hip, hooray! Hip, hip, hooray!" Lauren and Andie stood up and whooped loudly. Grabbing Jina's wrist, Lauren pulled her to her feet.

"Hip, hip, hooray!" Jina joined in happily.

Maybe friendships weren't always easy— but they were sure worth it!

**Don't miss the next book
in the Riding Academy series:
#12: LAUREN RIDES
TO THE RESCUE**

"Whisper!" Lauren eagerly unlatched the bottom stall door. "I've got a carrot for you!"

"A carrot?" a sharp voice said. "You know you're not supposed to feed the horses treats."

Lauren stopped dead in the doorway. A blond girl stood beside Whisper. She was frowning.

"I'm Melanie Harden," the girl said. "Remember? I'm a friend of your sister's and president of the Horse Masters Club."

Lauren gulped. "Oh. Hi. I, uh, forgot you were riding Whisper now."

Melanie stroked the mare's muzzle. "Yup. I might buy her, too. Then I could take her to college with me next year."

Tears filled Lauren's eyes. "She's really a special horse." Pulling the carrot from her pocket, she thrust it into Melanie's hand. "I just hope you love her as much as I do!" she blurted, and raced out of the barn.

ALISON HART has been horse-crazy since she was five years old. Her first pony was a pinto named Ted.

"I rode Ted bareback because we didn't have a saddle small enough," she says.

Now Ms. Hart lives and writes in Mt. Sidney, Virginia, with her husband, two kids, two dogs, one cat, her horse, April, and another pinto pony named Marble. A former teacher, she spends much of her time visiting schools to talk to her many Riding Academy fans. And you guessed it—she's still horse-crazy!